Country Girls

By Blake Karrington

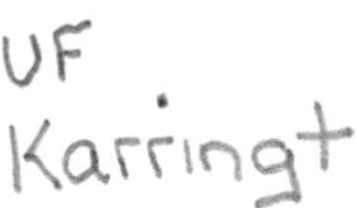

Country Girls

PUBLISHER'S NOTE:

This book is a work of fiction. Names, characters, businesses, organizations, places, events and incidents are the product of the author's imagination or are used fictionally. Any resemblance of actual persons, living or dead, events, or locales is entirely coincidental.

Contents

Chapter 1

Prada waited patiently on Oaklawn road for Niya to pull up. She'd been attentively watching the traffic that was going in and out of the trap house a block away. She was very familiar with the house, considering it belonged to Mayo, a nigga she'd been involved with for about two weeks now. Within that short period of time, she had gained intel on damn near his whole drug operation. Damn, I got that pussy that would make a nigga give up his whole paper route, Prada thought to herself.

The lights from a car pulling up and parking right behind her caught her attention. Niya stepped out of the all-black, 1995 Impala. She tucked the P.80 mm Ruger in her front pocket as she headed for Prada's car. She scanned the area thoroughly before she jumped into the passenger seat.

"Damn bitch, what took you so long?" Prada joked as she kept her eyes glued to the binoculars.

"Mommy business," Niya shot back. "I didn't even have time to shower," she joked.

"You nasty," Prada chuckled. "Look, in like twenty minutes, home-boy is gonna pull up and park the car. As soon as he goes into the house, just get in the car and pull off," Prada explained, passing her a set of keys.

"How much you think is in there?" Niya asked, taking a piece of gum out of her pocket and placing it in her mouth, as if what she was about to do meant nothing to her. In fact, it honestly didn't. Niya had made up her mind a long time ago that once she decided to take something, it belonged to her, and was there for the taking whenever she was ready.

"I'm not sure, but I know Mayo is about to re-up in the next couple of days, and this is his main trap house," Prada told her.

The all-white BMW 760 pulled up and parked a few doors away from the trap house, just as Prada said. The driver took a minute to get out of the car, but when he did, it was obvious why. He was having a short conversation with the passenger of the vehicle, an unknown female.

"Aaahhh shit! He got somebody else in the car!" Prada said. She wasn't expecting anybody else to be with him.

The female in the car didn't pose a threat, but Prada wasn't taking any chances with her. She couldn't risk her making a scene when Niya jumped in the car. If Mayo's worker even thought something was going on, he would surely come out of the house shooting.

"Let's get out of here," Prada said, starting her car up.

"What? Bitch you must be crazy," Niya said, with a serious look on her face. "We here now."

Niya pulled the P80 Rugger out and cocked a bullet into the chamber. For her, it was too late in the game to be turning back. She got out of the car, tucked the gun into her pocket, and fixed her clothes. She waited until the driver of the BMW got out of the car before she made her move.

"When I get up to the passenger door, pull my car right up next to his," Niya said, tossing Prada the keys to the Impala through the windows.

Niya proceeded to the car, just as the worker entered the house. Prada thought Niya had lost her mind as she watched her walk down the street. She quickly snapped out of her trance and headed for Niya's car.

Tap, Tap, Tap! A knock at the window caught the young woman's attention. She looked up and saw Niya standing there with a pleasant smile on her face. She appeared to be no danger at all to the young girl. As soon as she rolled the window down, Niya's whole demeanor changed.

"It ain't worth your life, baby girl, so just do what I say," Niya said, sticking the gun into the window and pointing it right at the girl's chest.

Just then, Prada pulled the Impala right next to the car. The young girl was so shook, she didn't know what to do. The only thing that she could do was comply, and that, she did. Niya quickly escorted her out of the BMW, but not before giving her a quick pat down.

"Go. Meet me at the spot," she told Prada, tapping the driver side door. Niya jumped in the passenger's seat of the white British Sedan. She placed the gun on her lap and waited for the owner to return.

"Where da fuck did she go?" Chad mumbled to himself, looking over at the clock.

He was sure he'd fucked Niya good enough to put her to sleep, but it was he who actually nodded off. If it wasn't for one of the kids waking up and coming into the room, Chad probably would still be asleep. He reached for his phone and dialed her cell, but it went straight to voicemail.

"11:00 at night," he mumbled as he walked over to the bedroom window.

He looked down and could see that her Range Rover was still in the driveway. That made him even more curious. He tried her number again, but it went straight to voicemail for the second time.

"Ya Mommy gonna make me kill her," Chad joked with Jahmil as he picked him up and walked back over to the bed.

Dro swung the book bag over his shoulder as he exited the house and went straight for the trunk. He looked up and down the block before popping the trunk open and tossing the bag inside. He didn't even notice the change of occupants in his car seat. He jumped in shock when the barrel of Niya's gun was jammed into his side. It was at that point that he looked over and realized that it wasn't Lexus.

"Play hero and I'll rearrange everything inside of you," Niya threatened, getting Dro's full attention. "Now pull off nice and easy," she directed, only wanting to get from in front of the trap house.

"You can't be serious, shawty," Dro said in a nonchalant manner. "You really th—"

Niya shoved the gun further in his gut, making him swallow the rest of his words. Not only did he swallow his words, he put the car in drive and pulled off, just as she said. They didn't go far, though. Once around the corner, Niya made him pull over and park. After searching his waist for any guns, Niya made him get out of the car with his hands raised over his head. Inside the trunk were three book bags and another large duffle bag. She quickly scanned the three book bags and saw that there was money inside.

"You know who shit you fuckin' wit, shawty?" Dro asked, as if he was surprised that anybody would mess with Mayo's money.

"To be honest with you, I really don't give a fuck," Niya told Dro before slamming the trunk.

She walked over and kicked Dro in the back of the knees, causing him to buckle. "You might wanna kill yaself while you're at it, shawty," Dro said, staring Niya in her face as she got into the driver's seat. "Kill yaself! Kill yaself," he yelled, watching Niya pull off.

Faces and names were always changing in the drug game. For now, the south side of Charlotte was in the possession of a young nigga named Dallaz. Ever since he could remember, he wanted to get money like the old heads. Throughout his teenage years, he watched as the OGs caused havoc in the hood.

"Damn, what's up Cuzo?" Ralph said walking up to the corner. "I see you out here on the late night."

"Yeah, lil nigga. I'm out here making sure dis money right. You know don't shit come to a sleeper, but a dream, ya dig," Dallaz said, passing Ralph the blunt of haze.

The whole time he stood there talking to Ralph, Dallaz kept his eyes on the traffic of crackheads walking up and down the street. Dallaz had the block running like an assembly line, and he made sure that this was a cop-and-roll spot. This wasn't a hang-out or a smoke place, it was a business, and he ran it with an iron fist. This had made him one of Mayo's top lieutenants.

Niya crept into the house as quietly as she could. She looked up at the clock on the wall in the living room, and noticed it was 1:35 in the morning.

"Shit," she mumbled to herself, knowing beyond a shadow of a doubt that Chad was upstairs waiting for her.

She headed for the basement, hoping that she could put the large duffle bag in her little stash spot. She moved as fast as she could, but the sounds of Chad calling her name from upstairs made her change course. The guns in the bag made more noise than she'd expected.

"Oh shit, Chad!" she yelled, scared to death when she made it to the top of the stairs, and he was standing right there. "You scared da shit out of me, boy."

"Where da fuck was you at?" Chad asked with an attitude, curiously looking down into the basement.

"Prada had troubles with her man tonight. I didn't even notice the time, boo," she answered, thinking fast on her feet. "We went and got some drinks at the b—"

"Well why da fuck didn't you answer ya phone?" he snapped, interrupting her before she could get the lie out. "And don't you gotta go the fuck to work in the morning?"

Niya pulled her cell phone from her pocket and passed it to Chad. She had put it on vibrate, then made Prada call it back to back so that the battery would die. It worked, because Chad couldn't even get the phone on.

"Don't worry boo, I'll be up in time to get back to work," she told Chad, grabbing the dead phone from his hand.

Niya hated lying to Chad. It weighed heavy on her heart because she loved him so much. They never kept secrets from each other, but the second life Niya was living couldn't be exposed to the love of her life. No matter how she put it, Chad would never understand, and if he told her to stop, 9 times out of 10, she would. That was something that Niya was trying to avoid.

"Are the kids asleep?" she asked, trying to change the mood in the room.

Chad just turned around and walked up the stairs, not really feeling like talking. Niya could tell that he was upset, but it was a tough pill she had to swallow for right now. As she walked up the stairs behind him, she felt the bulge in her back pocket. She reached back and her fingers touched the P.80 Ruger. She stopped in the middle of her stride. The gun was a vicious reminder of the kind of double life she was leading.

The entire room was deathly quiet; you could hear a mouse piss on cotton. Mayo sat on top of the piano in his living room, while JR, Made and Spice sat on the large sectional. Dro, the man at the head, sat in a little fold-up chair in the middle of the room. Not only did he feel totally embarrassed, but he also felt scared. Scared because he really didn't know what Mayo was going to do to him.

"So my nigga, run dis shit down one more time about what happened," Mayo said, jumping down off the piano.

Dro did as he was told, and broke down detail by detail, what had happened to him the night before. JR and Made laughed at him as he explained how he let a female catch him slippin. He even chuckled at how dumb it sounded. Mayo was probably the only nigga in the room that wasn't smiling. Whoever it was that robbed Dro, had robbed him, and 140K lost left no room for laughter in Mayo's heart.

"Ahh you think it's funny right? You think it's a joke you let a bitch rob you, my nigga?" Mayo evilly chuckled as he walked over to Dro. "You got 140K right now to pay me back nigga?" he asked, pulling a large .357 Magnum from his waist.

"Nah May, it wasn't even like that homie," Dro answered, now looking at Mayo with fear in his eyes.

Mayo walked around behind Dro, took a step back, and pointed the gun at the back of his head. Dro could feel the hairs on the back of his neck stand up. The sound of the hammer being cocked back confirmed what was about to happen. Dro just closed his eyes. Everybody in the room tensed up, but before Mayo could pull the trigger, the front door opened and Prada walked in. Everyone in the turned to see who it was, even Dro.

Prada entered in time to witness a murder. Mayo never took his eyes off Prada as he pulled the trigger. The loud blast from the large revolver made everyone jump. The bullet tore through Dro's skull and planted itself in the center of his brain, killing him instantly. His body slumped over and fell to the floor. Prada stood there in shock, not knowing what to do. This was the first time she'd ever experienced something like this, and she wasn't sure if Mayo was going to do the same thing to her. She quickly got it together and came to the conclusion that she had to play the situation like an old mob housewife.

She walked over to Mayo, looked down at Dro's body, then back up at him. "Have this shit cleaned up before dinner," she said, motioning with her finger as if it didn't faze her. "Chicken or steak?" she asked Mayo before kissing him on the cheek and walking off towards the kitchen.

Mayo just smiled as he responded, "Chicken, you know a nigga trying to chill on that red meat." He watched Prada walk off, thinking to himself that he had finally copped a winner. Mayo knew he needed a strong bitch on his team, one who understood what he was into and didn't have a problem playing her position.

Niya had the kids up and ready for daycare before Chad cracked his eyes open. It seemed like his dick woke up before him, because he was rock hard. The smell of bacon and eggs flooded the whole house, and after washing his face and brushing his teeth, Chad headed downstairs to the war zone. The twins sat in their high-chairs making a complete mess out of their breakfast, while Niya juggled between talking on the phone, watching the news on the kitchen television, and preparing Chad's plate. It was chaos, but the regular morning ritual for the Stafford family.

"Good morning to you too," Niya said, hanging up the phone and bringing Chad's plate to the table.

"Good morning, shawty," he responded, then turned his attention to the twins.

"Oh I'm shawty this morning, huh?" It was obvious that he was still upset about last night. "So how long are you going to be mad at me, Chad? I said that I was sorry," Niya whined.

"I'ma be mad until I get over the fact that you walked in this house at 1:30 in the morning —"

"I told you I was with Prada," she said, cutting him off.

"Yeah that's what you say," Chad responded as he wiped the food from baby Khoula's face.

"So what's that supposed to mean, Chad? Are you insinuating something? I mean, it's obvious you don't believe me, so why don't you say what's really on ya mind?"

Chad didn't say another word. He really didn't feel like arguing this morning, and he knew that if he really said what was on his mind, it would have gotten ugly. He did what any man in his right mind would do. He simply got up from the table and took his food upstairs.

Prada sat in the bathroom on the edge of the tub with her face buried in her hands. She still couldn't believe she had witnessed Mayo killing somebody. The tears poured down her face, and it wasn't because she was afraid, but because she felt somewhat responsible for Dro's death. She never thought in a million years that Mayo would take it that far.

"Prada! Prada!" Mayo yelled out as he walked into the bedroom. The voice alone startled her, causing Prada to jump up and grab a washrag for her face. She quickly splashed some water on her face just as he opened the bathroom door.

"You alright in here, ma?" Mayo asked with a curious look on his face.

"Yeah, I'm good, baby. I was just washing up. Did you take care of that downstairs, yet?" she asked, referring to Dro's dead body.

"It's being taken care of as we speak. I wanted to talk to you about that too."

"You don't have to explain," Prada said, cutting him off. "You did what you had to do, I'm sure."

"Naw, ma. That's something you didn't have to witness. It's just that when it comes to my money, I have zero tolerance for incompetence," Mayo tried to explain.

Prada wasn't trying to hear any of that. It went in one ear and out the other. Her mind was made up the moment she saw Dro's body slumped over. This short relationship was over, and it wasn't anything Mayo could do to make things right. Prada was already prepared to have the conversation with Niya and let her know, she was done spying on Mayo.

Chapter 2

Gwen dropped the last nine ounces of powder into the Pyrex pot that was sitting on the stove. She was a chef when it came to cooking crack, and there weren't too many people in North Carolina that could mess with her. That was one of the reasons JR loved her so much. That and the fact that she was sexy as hell.

"Pass me the ice," Gwen told JR as she continued to whip the baking soda in with the cocaine."

JR brought the ice over to the sink, and then slid up behind Gwen. He wrapped his arms around her waist. A soft kiss to the back of her neck gave her the chills.

"You better stop before I fuck this money up," she joked, scraping the thick liquid from around the edges of the pot.

With her skills, it was impossible for her to mess up the product. Hell, she learned how to cook coke from the best, her son's father. It had been a while since her and Chad had actually been together, but many good jewels stuck with her that she learned from him. Making crack was one of them.

"It's me and you this weekend?" JR asked Gwen, grabbing her and pressing her fat ass up against his dick.

"I don't know. I got to see if Zion's Dad can take him. You know that's gonna be a slim chance," she answered as she took the pot of cocaine off the stove and placed it into the sink.

Gwen and JR had been together for about a year, and ever since the day Chad found out Gwen was in love with another man, their relationship had gone south. It was as if they had become enemies. They couldn't get along for anything, not even for the sake of little Zion, their only child together.

"Well look, if he don't want to take his son, then maybe we can bring him along with us," JR suggested. "It can be like a family outing," he said, planting yet another kiss to the back of her neck.

Gwen dumped the ice and some cold water into the pot of crack, and then turned around to face JR. She had to admit to herself that she had love for him, it just wasn't the crazy love she once had for Chad. However, JR had come into her life when she needed somebody the most. Outside of being one of the most vicious niggas to come out of Charlotte, he was also kind and sweet when it came down to Gwen. He was everything a woman looked for in a man; a rough shell, but soft inside. It was no doubt that she really cared about him, but at the same time, Gwen wasn't stupid enough to play the family card with JR.

Chad was a hop, skip, and a jump away, and even though Chad had given up the street life and had a new family of his own, she knew that he was an extremely proud man. If the word got back from the streets that some other man was out there playing father to his child, it would not sit well with him. Gwen was well aware of Chad's temper and had witnessed more than her share of his wrath on those he perceived to be his enemies. No, Gwen thought to herself, sometimes it's best not to wake a sleeping giant. If she and JR were going out this weekend, it would be without Zion.

"Niya is gonna kill us if we can't get this building," Diamond said, looking around the empty warehouse.

Diamond's phone began to ring. She excused herself from her friend, Tiffany, and the realtor who was showing them around.

"Hey girl, what's up wit the buildings? How do it look?" Niya asked as she jumped into her car.

"Girl, this place is big as shit. It's more than enough space, plus it got a second level to it."

Niya smiled at the description Diamond was giving her about the place. It had always been her dream to own her own club, and for the past few months, she'd been working towards that goal. That was just one of the reasons why she started taking money from big time drug dealers around North Carolina. Niya was more than determined. This was the come up she and Chad needed in their lives. Both of them had taken on jobs just to make ends meet, and currently that's all they were doing. Also, she had the girls of her crew to think about. How long would they be able to continue doing this? "No, this is the only way out, and I have to make it happen," Niya uttered to herself.

"So what do the numbers look like?" Niya asked, looking back at the house before pulling out of the driveway.

Diamond was quiet on the phone for a minute before she spoke. "They want 1.5 million for this building, Niya, and they are not taking anything less than that," Diamond explained. "Where the hell are you going to get 1.5 million from, Niya?" she asked with little doubt in her tone.

"Don't worry about it D, we're gonna get it," Niya assured. "If I got to rob every Nigga in North Carolina, it's gonna get done fo sho," Niya said.

"Big sis, we also got another problem," Diamond said, letting out a sigh of frustration. "The realtor said that he can only hold this building for another 30 days. If we can't come up with the money by then, he's gonna sell the building.

"Damn," Niya mumbled to himself.

Thirty days wasn't enough time for Niya to come up with that type of money, and she knew it. Given the couple of jobs she and Prada had lined up, it was possible she could come up with a half million. At times like this, she wished that Chad was still in the game, because 1.5 million would have been paid by the end of the day.

"Diamond, I need more time. I can get the money, I just need more time," she pled. "Just see what you can do," she told Diamond before hanging up the phone.

Gwen watched as the traffic light changed from green to yellow, but at her rate of speed, she wasn't going to be able to stop the car. The only thing she could to do was go through the red light. Everything seemed ok, until she saw lights flashing behind her.

"Fuck," she mumbled to herself, thinking about what was in the car.

Today was Gwen's day to deliver all the drugs to the multiple trap houses that JR had in the hood. She had enough crack in the trunk to trigger a federal indictment, not to mention the 9mm she had tucked away under her seat. Gwen's anxiety was at an all-time high as she pulled the car over. After about a minute or two, the officer got out of the police cruiser and approached Gwen's car. His partner walked up to the passenger side. Slowly and calmly, Gwen reached for her sun visor to grab her license and registration.

"Did I do something wrong, officer?" Gwen asked with an innocent look on her face.

"You ran a red light ma'am. Can I see your license and registration, with proof of insurance?" the officer said, while taking a good look around the inside of Gwen's car.

She complied, giving the officer all of her info. The second cop was making Gwen extremely nervous. He stayed behind, while his partner went back to the cruiser to run the paperwork. He asked question after question, mainly pertaining to where Gwen was coming from and where she was going. The whole time he was questioning her, he was looking around the car in a suspicious manner. Gwen just kept her cool. She had been schooled by Chad, and knew that a routine traffic stop alone was not probable cause to search the car. For now, she was in the clear... unless the K-9 unit showed up.

Chapter 3

"What's good wit you, homie?" JR said giving Mayo daps as they walked through the door. JR and Mayo had been friends since grade school, and there wasn't too much they didn't know about each other

"I needed to holler at you about the bull Dro told me before I checked him out," Mayo said as both men took a seat on the couch.

JR could feel that Mayo was on to something, and he knew that Mayo wasn't going to forget about his money. He couldn't let it go, and he was determined to get down to the bottom of who took 140k from him. "Dro told me that when the chick was robbing him, he noticed a tattoo on her wrist. It said "MHB" inside some crazy little sign," Mayo explained.

JR's brain went into overdrive. It was only one person he knew of that had a similar tattoo. It was the last person he thought would have had something to do with the robbery, but a clear vision of the tattoo "MHB" was on Gwen's right ankle. He remembered Gwen telling him a little bit about the tattoo when they first started dating, but he couldn't remember what it stood for.

"You sure the nigga said it was on her wrist?" JR asked.

"Yeah, and he said she had another tat on her arm, but he couldn't make it out."

Prada crept out of the bedroom and down the hall to the top of the steps. She could hear Mayo and JR talking about the situation with the robbery, and wanted to see just how much Mayo knew. She had missed a lot of the conversation, but heard all she needed to hear from Mayo.

"Yo homie, if it's the last thing I do, I'ma find dis bitch who took my money and I'ma blow her fuckin' head off." Mayo declared with determination in his eyes.

Prada almost choked on her own spit when she heard that. She feared that Mayo might know more than she thought he did. She slowly backed up from the top of the steps and went back into the bedroom.

"Damn homie, I'ma put my ears to the streets, ASAP," JR said, giving Mayo daps before getting up from the couch.

As he was leaving the house, the only thing he could think about was Gwen, and if she knew anything about the robbery. One thing he did know for sure was that Mayo was going to find out who did it. He recalled the time when he and Mayo were in middle school, and a high school kid by the name of Art, beat Mayo up and took his lunch money for about a month straight. When Mayo got old enough and started playin around with guns, he sought Art out, robbed him, beat him up, and then shot him in his face. JR could remember Mayo's words the day after he killed Art. It wasn't about the fact that he beat me up, I killed him cause he took my lunch money! JR knew that Mayo's determination was going to make him victorious in finding the culprit behind the robbery.

Chad knew the storm was coming; he could feel it in the air. As he opened his front door to leave for work, Gwen was pulling up. She was worse than a storm, she was his Baby Momma/ex-wifey. Before he met Niya, Gwen was his everything and the relationship they had was the kind that dreams were made of. They were like the modern day Bonnie and Clyde. During that time, Chad ran Charlotte in the drug game, but a single bullet to the side of his head put him in early retirement. He knew that he was lucky to survive it, and after beating a federal case, Chad recognized the blessing God had shown him and decided to give up the life and go square.

He got a job with the City of Charlotte, and had been laying concrete for the last two years. He loved Gwen, but he knew she wasn't the type for a regular Joe blow. Gwen wanted the glamorous life, and everything that came with it. Gwen had more aggression and drive than most men did. After Gwen left, Chad made a life decision and chose Niya, the calmer of the two to build a future with. He knew that having a relationship with Niya would cause a lifelong vendetta with Gwen. She and Niya had been close at one time. They both grew up in Clanton Park and were classmates through elementary, middle, and high school. Chad knew that he couldn't end up with some soft broad, because Gwen would constantly run over her, until she had run her away. He knew that although Niya was calm, she was at heart, a very dangerous woman when provoked.

Niya was light skinned, with long hair, and had to constantly prove herself growing up in the hood. Some girl's boyfriend was always liking her and this would keep her in a fight. Her hand game was crazy. One time, a girl pulled down on her. Niya grabbed the gun and began beating the girl un-mercifully, until one of the other girls drew another pistol and fired a shoot to get Niya to stop. Well, she obviously didn't know who she was dealing with, because Niya walked up to her, grabbed her gun as well, and fired a bullet into the young woman's leg.

She stood over her and asked, "You happy now? You got what you wanted. I stopped whooping her ass, and all it cost you was a leg!" From that day forward, everyone in Southside knew that Niya was a sleeping giant which no one wanted to wake.

"What seems to be ya problem, Chad?" Gwen began yelling before she even got out of the car. "You haven't seen ya fuckin' son in a month," she continued, slamming the car door behind her.

"Come on Gwen, wit da bullshit. I told you I been busy," he shot back.

"Too busy to see ya own fuckin son?"

"Look man, you know a nigga out here working, and I got to take all the overtime I can get. You can bring him over here next weekend," he said, flagging her off and heading for his car.

"You sad, Chad. Ya son need you—"

"I'm sad? I'm the one out here breaking my fucking back with this concrete. You cleaning up real good wit the amount of money you get for child support, and I'm sad?" Chad said, cutting her off. "I'm sure you got JP ...JT...J whatever doin' a good job playin daddy," he said as he got into his car.

Chad really didn't mean the last statement, but he knew that he was getting underneath Gwen's skin, which was exactly what he wanted to do.

He isn't the only one who could play this game, Gwen thought to herself. "Oh I'm glad you ok with that, because JR wanted to take him on a father son trip this weeke—" She didn't even have time to get the words out her mouth before Chad was out of the car and standing in her face with his hand on her chin.

"Gwen, don't you ever play with me like that. You tell that nigga to take his own fucking son, you hear me?" Chad uttered through clenched teeth. He shook Gwen's head up and down for her. Chad gave her a light tap on her cheek and got back into his car and pulled away.

Diamond pulled up to the realtor's office, hoping to catch Mike before he left for the day. She needed to get the extension so that Niya could have enough time to come up with the money to buy the building. When she got to the front door, it was locked, but the lights were on. She looked down at her watch and saw that it was a little after 5:00.

Just as she was about to turn around and leave, she caught a glimpse of someone moving around in the back. It was Mike leaving his office and going across the hall into the copy room. Diamond knocked on the glass to catch his attention.

"Hey Diamond, I was just about to leave," Mike said, opening the door. "What can I do for you?"

"I know it's kinda late, but I really need to talk to you about the building," she pleaded with a sad, puppy dog face.

Mike stepped to the side and let her into the office. For a second, he couldn't take his eyes off her. Diamond had a way of letting her body speak for her. Standing at 5 feet 6 inches, weighing 155lbs, 34-B breast, a curvy waist, flat stomach and a nice petite ass, Diamond was the reason white men lusted over black women the way they did. Mike was no exception. Diamond's light brown skin complemented her long, curly, black hair that stopped at her shoulders. Today, it was pulled back into a ponytail, bringing out the beauty of her face.

"I really need ya help," Diamond said, sitting her large, brown leather print Gucci bag on his desk. "I really need additional time to buy the building. I know that I can have the money in a couple of months."

"I'm sorry Diamond. I have someone looking at the building in a couple of days. I won't be able to hold it if he's ready to buy it," Mike explained.

"Come on Mike," she whined, walking around to his side of the desk and taking a seat on the edge of it in front of him. Her sweetly scented body drove Mike into freak mode. He damn near started to drool, looking at the way her thighs were kissing each other in those jeans. Diamond noticed the attention he was giving her body and decided to entice him some more.

"Sixty days is all I need," Diamond said in a seductive manner, lifting one of her legs up and planting her Zegna heels on his armrest.

Mike got up from his chair, and at first, Diamond thought she had messed up. Then, he put his hand on her thigh. He stood between her legs, looking down at her with lust-filled eyes.

"How far are you willing to go?" he said in his most seductive, yet playful tone.

Diamond knew right then, that she was going to have to take one for the team. She reached for Mike's belt and unfastened his buckle, while getting off the desk and taking a seat in his chair. Mike's dick was rock hard before his pants hit the floor, and before he knew it, Diamond was taking his white flesh into her mouth. The warmth of her mouth caused him to lean against his desk. His eyes rolled to the back of his head as Diamond completely devoured his dick. He could feel the head of his manhood tapping the back of her moistened throat, and the sounds of spit splashing around in her mouth heightened the sensitivity of his dick.

Mike couldn't help but to grab the back of her head as she continued to suck. He could feel the tingling sensation in the pit of his stomach, and he knew he was about to nut. He quickly grabbed a handful of her hair and pulled Diamond off his dick. It sounded like a suction cup releasing its pressure when she let his dick go. He pulled her up to him and kissed her.

In the heat of the moment, Diamond returned his kiss, stuffing her tongue in his mouth. With one hand, Mike reached down and unfastened Diamond's jeans. His other hand spun her around and bent her over onto the desk. Within seconds, Mike was pushing his meat inside of Diamond's pink-box. She spread her legs apart, and loosened up her walls so that she could take all of him inside of her. Mike slammed his meat deeper into her. Her loud moans resounded throughout the empty office as Mike continued pounding and pounding away.

Niya sat on her bed counting all of the money that she had in her stash. The bed was full of 50's, 20's, 10's, and single dollar bills. She could tell that the money she's been taking was drug money, just by how dirty the bills looked. So far, and including the recent take for 140k, that she and Prada split, she had a little more than 300k. The whole time she was counting the money, she thought about the club she wanted to own. "1.5 million," she mumbled to herself shaking her head.

Niya was still within reach of being able to set up a mortgage for the property, but she really wanted to buy it straight out, with no strings attached. Niya was so caught up with counting the money, she didn't hear Chad pull up, nor did she hear him come into the house.

Chad tried to be quiet, thinking that everyone was taking a nap. He knew that Niya was there, because her truck was still outside. As he crept up the stairs, he could hear some noises coming from his room. It was a familiar sound to him, and as he got closer to his bedroom, he knew that it was money being counted. The door was cracked open just enough for Chad to see Niya sitting on the bed with a handful of money. He started to just bust through the door and demand an explanation, but decided against it. He calmly backed up and headed back downstairs.

Where da fuck did she get all that money? he thought to himself, pacing back and forth in the kitchen.

One thing Chad learned from being in the streets is that things are rarely what they seem. So, before he allowed himself to confront

Niya while he was upset, he would just let it be for now. One thing was for sure, and two things for certain; this wasn't going to be the end of it.

"Yo, what's wrong wit you?" Mayo asked Prada, who was lying in bed with her back to him.

He felt that something wasn't right ever since he killed Dro in front of her, and he was really unsure how he was going to deal with the situation.

"I'm good, May," she responded. "I'm just a little tired.

"Yeah, what you pregnant or something?" he asked, sliding up behind her and placing his arm around her waist.

That comment was enough to get her attention. She turned around and gave him a curious look. *I hope this nigga ain't tryna get me pregnant,* she thought to herself.

She had to admit that the sex was good, and there were a couple of instances where she felt him cum inside of her. But, there was no way she should or would be feeling symptoms of pregnancy. They had only known each other for about a month, and started having sex three weeks ago. After a week of safe sex, she let him go inside of her raw. All of this information played back in her head for a split second.

"Boy, don't be tryna jinx me. I'm not tryna have no babies right now," Prada joked. "Don't make me have to put a rubber on you," she said smiling.

"Ah shawty, dis daddy pussy now," he shot back, climbing on top of her. "You got my nose wide open," he chuckled leaning in to kiss her soft lips.

He hadn't lied when he said that he was open. Prada had done some things to him that women only do with their husbands, not to mention the fact that she was probably the toughest red-bone in Charlotte. She was pretty as all outdoors. Her natural eye color was a goldish-brown and she really didn't have to smile in order to see her dimples. Her hair reached to the center of her back, and her 5'7", 170lb frame was stacked in all the right places. 38D breasts, thick thighs, fat ass, and a smile that can make heaven open up the gates.

It wasn't hard for Mayo to fall for someone like Prada, and if Prada wasn't focused the way that she was, she probably would have fallen for him as well. He was everything she liked physically. Tall, dark, and handsome. He even had the nerve to have a full head of naturally curly hair. It wasn't too many niggas in Charlotte with curly hair. Prada just had the ability to control her emotions and not get attached. Prada's only mission in life right now was to gain the last two digits to Mayo's safe, take everything in it, then move on to the next nigga. That was what she did. She was an "MHB" girl and would be that until the death of her.

Chapter 4

Prada pulled into the strip mall where she was supposed to meet up with Niya for their Tuesday ritual at a small eatery. The white Range Rover sitting in front of the store confirmed that Prada was late again. But with what she had to tell Niya, being late would be the last thing they talked about.

"Girl dis nigga is crazy as shit," Prada began as she pushed the plate of food Niya had ordered to the side like it wasn't even there. "He killed that boy right in front of me," she whispered with her hands cupped around her mouth.

"What? Bitch you better get the hell out of there," Niya told her with a concerned look on her face. "Dat nigga might kill you next."

"Shit, I'm one digit away from having the combo to his safe. And when I say safe, it look like a walk-in closet," Prada said, snapping her neck back and forth.

Niya had to chuckle at Prada and the way she was trying to look so ghetto. Through everything she had seen Mayo do, she was still in it to win it. Niya admired that part about her.

"You MHB," Niya said, smiling and shaking her head.

"Oh shit that reminds me, the nigga we robbed told him he saw a "MHB" tattoo on ya wrist. Mayo was making all kinds of threats about how he was goin to get to the bottom of it," Prada added.

The Money Hungry Bitches consisted of Diamond, Tiffany, Tiki, Lisa, who had died in a car accident, and lastly, Niya's best friend turned archenemy, Gwen. Prada was a new MHB, but she hadn't gotten her tattoo yet. She was waiting for the right time to get it, and now definitely wasn't the time.

Niya was in deep thought, thinking about the first day that she had met Prada, and how far she had come from being that timid, helpless, little girl. They were both sitting in the lobby of the abortion clinic. Niya had gotten pregnant by her high school sweetheart when she was 15 years old. She knew it was no way she was going to be able to tell her saved and sanctified grandmother, whom she lived with, that she was having sex, and was pregnant. She knew that her grandmother would ship her off quickly, before she let Niya embarrass her to the whole neighborhood and church congregation. So, Niya did the only thing she could think of, and that was to steal the $400.00 from the money her grandmother kept in her sock drawer and handle her business.

She convinced her boyfriend at the time to give her a ride to the appointment, since he was seventeen and old enough to drive. While in the waiting room, she could hear Prada on the phone, crying and arguing with someone about coming to pick her up, especially since they hadn't given her any money to help. Niya stepped in, and ever since that day, Prada had been at her side.

"So now what?" Prada asked, looking over at the stress in her best friend's eyes. Whatever Niya wanted to do, Prada was down with it. That's just the kind of love and loyalty she had for MHB. She also knew the love Niya had for her, and that whatever she decided was in the best interest of all.

"Hurry up and get that last digit to that safe," Niya instructed before digging her fork into her lunch. Niya hated the fact she had to put her girl back in harm's way. However, she also knew that if she didn't make this club dream a reality soon, they would never be able to stop with this lifestyle. Therefore, it was better to take this chance now, for a safer future.

Gwen was sitting at the kitchen table weighing and bagging up ounces and half ounces of crack, when JR came through the door. Although JR was pretty much the supplier, Gwen was the engine of the car. Gwen moved most of the coke JR bought. She knew pretty much every drug dealer in Charlotte, along with all the hot spots for heavy crackhead traffic. That was all courtesy of Chad, who had her in the passenger seat the whole time he flooded the streets, back in his day.

"Yo, I need to talk to you about something," JR said sincerely as he came into the kitchen and took a seat at the table with her.

From the way he sounded, Gwen thought someone had died. He was only like this when it was something serious. "What's up, babe?" she said, turning the scale off.

"I need you to tell me everything you know about MHB," he said with a serious look in his eyes.

That caught Gwen by surprise. She couldn't understand why he would suddenly be asking about MHB, considering the fact that Gwen hardly ever talked about the tattoo on her ankle.

"Why, what's going on JR?" Gwen asked with a curious look on her face.

JR began to explain the whole situation with Mayo and the money. He told her about Dro and his story of being robbed. JR explained that Dro had told Mayo about the tattoo he had seen on the female who robbed him, and how Mayo really just wanted to get his money back. JR wasn't speaking in a harsh manner, but rather in a concerned tone, something Gwen picked up on the moment he sat down.

"So what do you wanna know, JR?" Gwen probed, trying to see where he was going with his line of questions.

"I wanna know everything. I wanna know everybody that's a part of MHB. Where they from, where they live, how many of ya'll there is, and most importantly, which chick got MHB tattooed on her right wrist," he said, scooting his chair closer to Gwen.

Even though Gwen didn't mess with the people in MHB, that didn't take away the fact that she was still an MHB herself. The rules and regulations still applied in Gwen's life, and it didn't matter what the situation was, she could never cross her MHB family. It was more about who she was, and less about what had transpired. So she responded as if she was at the last meeting.

"Look, I don't know what you plan on doing, but I haven't been a part of MHB for years, boo. Even if I did have info on them, I couldn't possibly get involved."

Gwen wasn't dumb at all. She knew that Mayo was going to kill whoever took his money, just as fast as he killed the person they took the money from. She couldn't have an MHB member's blood on her hands. No matter how much she hated Niya, she wasn't about to tell JR that she was the only member who had MHB tattooed on her right wrist.

JR could see that Gwen wasn't gonna budge, and was going to stand firm in her loyalty to her crew by any means necessary. The look she had was the same kind of look he would have if someone were to inquire about Mayo. JR was genuinely concerned about her, because he knew how far Mayo was willing to go about his money. Anybody from MHB was liable to get shot, and that included Gwen, if she wasn't careful.

Prada walked into the house to find Mayo already in his safe, putting the money in and taking cocaine out. Damn, she thought to herself. She was mad because she wasn't there to catch the last two numbers. All she could do was wait until he went back in it again, and when he did, she was going to be ready.

Chad had decided to spend some time with his son, instead of waiting for the weekend. He had been feeling guilty about the lack of time he'd been giving him, due to the rift he had with Gwen. It wasn't a question whether or not he loved his son, because he did. Zion was his first born, and a planned pregnancy with the woman he was in love with at the time. Zion wasn't an accident, or someone Chad had to learn how to love. His feelings for his boy came natural.

When Gwen pulled up to the house, Chad was already sitting outside waiting for them. It was rare that Gwen actually came to the house, and that was due to the constant tension between her and Niya. They couldn't stand each other, and Chad was the core of the problem.

"Daddy! Daddy!" Zion yelled, getting out of the car and running up to him.

The love he displayed for his father was so emotional, even Gwen had to smile. No amount of time away from each other could break their bond, and in some ways, Gwen respected that.

"Get out the car, I wanna holla at you for a minute," Chad told Gwen, catching her off guard.

"I don't have time, I got somewhere to go—" she tried to plead, only to pair of deaf ears.

"Get out the car G," he said again, cutting her off.

He hadn't called her by the name G since they were together, and that by itself compelled Gwen to get out of the car. Even though she had on something as simple as a pair of thigh-high shorts, a tank-top and some Alexander McQueen sandals, she still looked good. Chad's dick got hard at the thought of sliding between her thick thighs. He could just picture himself biting each thigh right before planting his face into her pussy.

"Yo, listen. This beef between me and you gotta stop. Let me be the first to apologize for everything that got us to this point," Chad began.

"Chad you don't have to —"

"Chill out shawty, let me talk," he said stopping her. "I'm not the same person I used to be. I changed a lot over the past couple of years, and I've come to realize what's important in life," he continued.

Just listening to him, Gwen could see the change in his attitude. He sounded like someone who was responsible and knew what he wanted out of life. He sounded like a person who had a heart and a conscience, and not like the thugged-out nigga she fell in love with. He sounded like a man, a real man.

"I just want you to know that I'm gonna do better. I'ma do all I can to be a better father," he said with all the humility in the world.

Gwen was stuck for a moment as she listened to him. She couldn't help but to think about how things would have been if they had never parted ways. In some odd way, she wished that she could have grown with him into being the kind of person he was today, but four years ago, Gwen wasn't ready to leave the life of a hustler's wife. Before Gwen could even get a chance to respond, the white Range Rover pulled into the driveway right behind her car, blocking her in.

Niya jumped out the truck, and it was obvious that she had an attitude because she didn't even speak to Gwen. Chad gave her a stern look as if to say, "don't start," as she walked and kissed him. Gwen just smiled, finding it funny that Niya thought the kiss made her jealous.

"Well look, I'm tryin' to leave. Can you move ya truck so I can go?" Gwen asked, breaking the awkward silence. "You know what... I do need to have a word or two with you," Gwen said, looking at Niya.

They both looked at Chad as if to dismiss him, so the women could talk. He was reluctant, knowing how ugly this conversation could get, but he chose to leave them alone anyway. He wasn't going far, though.

"I'll be over here," he said pointing to Zion who was sitting on the front steps.

The ladies were silent until Chad was out of hearing range. Niya didn't know what to expect, but she was ready for any physical confrontation Gwen was plotting.

"So when did MHB start robbing people?" Gwen asked with both an attitude and disappointment.

The question caught Niya off guard.

"What the hell are you talking about?" Niya shot back.

"Cut da shit, Ni, I know about the trap house that got robbed last week," Gwen said leaning against her car. "They say she had a MHB tat on her right wrist," she continued, grabbing Niya's right arm.

"You should mind ya fuckin' business," Niya shot back, snatching her arm away.

Niya was a little ashamed about what she was doing. MHB was never about violence when Tiki, an OG wife started it and passed it on to Niya and Gwen. It started as an empowerment movement for young women to take control of their lives and be more independent. It was over the course of time, that both Gwen and Niya changed the movement. MHB was transformed into a handful of young women who competed to see who could bag the most infamous drug dealers in North Carolina. Money hungry was just a better phrase to use than gold-diggers, because that's all they became, just at a higher level.

"You know, robbery is a new low for you, Ni," Gwen rubbed in, as she reached for her door. "If I was you ..."

"Well you're not me," Niya snapped back. "You do you, and let me do me," she said as she headed for the truck so that she could let Gwen out.

When Niya got into her car, a tap at her window got her attention. It was Gwen.

"What?" Niya said as she rolled the window down.

"You might want to cover that tattoo up before you end up having a hundred niggas runnin' up in ya house," Gwen warned.

That was going to be only warning Gwen would give her, and that was only due to her being a MHB. After waving to Zion and Chad, who were still sitting on the steps, Gwen jumped in her car and left.

Det. Butler walked into the wooded area just off the highway, where he was greeted by another detective, a female named Rose. Butler was led to the makeshift gravesite where Dro's body was being photographed by the forensic unit.

"A single shot to the back of his head. He didn't feel a thing," Det. Rose said, kneeling down next to the corpse.

Det. Butler reached into Dro's pockets, looking for identification. It was there along with some money and car keys. "I guess we can rule out robbery," Butler said, looking at the contents. "Jeffrey Davis," he announced holding the ID to his eyes.

It was simple murders like this that made Det. Butler want to be a cop. He grew up in Charlotte, and knew firsthand how violent the city was. He would do everything in his power to solve this case.

Chapter 5

Club Caviar was jam-packed, and it seemed that everyone from Charlotte was in the building. For MHB, it was ladies' night out, a well needed break from a long week of work. Diamond, Tiffany, and Niya sat in the VIP booth surrounded by bottles of Patron and Grey Goose. The oldest member of the crew, Tiki, was making her rounds in the club.

Tiki was the original founder of MHB, back in the day when the He-men crew ran the city. Tiki was married to the leader, and figured she would form a crew for the women of the male members. After her husband, Andre, was violently murdered, she decided to turn the group into a positive support group. After years of being in the midst of things, she decided to pass the torch to Gwen and Niya, when most of the He-men crew hung up their jerseys. Now, Tiki was more of an adviser than an actual member, but the people in the city still loved her.

"What you thinking about?" Niya yelled over the music to Diamond, who was lost in her thoughts.

She hadn't stopped thinking about Mike the realtor, and what happened in his office a few days ago. Most women would have felt bad and degraded for doing what she did, but Diamond liked the crazy wild office sex. Visions of Mike slamming her over on his desk and pounding her from the back raced through her mind.

"I got the extension," Diamond said, with a big smile on her face.

"90 days!" she yelled.

Niya was ecstatic. All she was
Diamond managed to get 90. Niya s
had on her face before she took a sip o

"How da hell did you get 90 da
having a feeling what Diamond was g

It was silent at the table for a second. Tiffany even stopped what she was doing to hear the answer. "I gave him a shot of pussy," Diamond laughed. Everybody at the table laughed at the surprising twist.

"You whore," Tiffany joked.

"Yo ass sittin' up there wit a big ole smile on ya face. Let me find out that white boy got ya ass sprung," Niya chimed in.

"Girl, he fucked me like a porn star," Diamond laughed, taking another sip of her drink. "I know he got some nigga in him."

They all burst out laughing again. Just as they finished laughing, Prada walked into the VIP section. She was rocking a black, sleeveless, Dolce and Gabbana pencil dress, and a pair of red and black Louis Vuitton, peep-toe heels. She could've been on the runway, because all eyes were on her. Niya admired the way Prada dressed when it was time to get fresh. But even with all that was going on in the club, Niya was still on point and aware of her surroundings. About fifteen steps behind Prada was a familiar face. At first she didn't know who or where she remembered the girl from, but as the female got closer, it was like a light bulb had switched on.

"The girl from the car," Niya mumbled to herself as she reached into her pocketbook.

It was hard to get guns inside of club Caviar, especially for a pocketknife almost always made it in. Through ces, Prada noticed the frown on Niya's face when . She had to think about it for a second, but quickly d who she had brought along. It was almost too late, Niya was climbing out of the booth, knife in hand and ng right at her target.

"Whoa! Whoa! Whoa! Sis it's cool," Prada yelled out, stepping in front of her.

"Oh shit!" Diamond yelled, seeing the knife in Niya's hand.

"What da fuck is going on here, Prada?" Niya yelled with rage still in her eyes.

"Let me explain... Wait, let me explain!" Prada shouted, putting the young girl behind her.

It took a minute for everyone to cool off, but eventually the dust settled.

Diamond, Tiffany, and Niya all stared at the girl standing behind Prada looking scared to death.

"She's only 16 years old Ni," Prada began. "She didn't have nowhere else to go, so I took her in and let her stay at my apartment," Prada explained.

"What was she doin' wit him?" Niya asked, talking about her being in the car with Dro.

"She was doing the same thing I was doing ten years ago, when I was her age," Prada answered with a sad look on her face.

Just saying those words brought tears to Prada's eyes, as a recap of her parentless childhood flashed through her head. The hard look in Niya's eyes also faded away, and was replaced with a bit of sorrow.

Niya knew the trials and tribulations that Prada had gone through. She herself, had experienced firsthand how cold the streets could be for a young girl. At the age of 16, Niya and pretty much everyone at the table knew the struggle. It was grown ass men like Dro who took advantage of a teenage girls with nobody to look out for them. For those reasons, Niya became a little more understanding.

"What's your name?" Niya asked, folding the knife up and putting it back in her bag.

"I'm Alexus," the young girl said, coming from behind Prada.

"Yeah, and Alexus got a birthday coming up in about twenty-minutes," Prada announced with a big smile. "I was hoping she could bring in her 17th birthday with us."

It got quiet at the table for what seemed like forever. The only thing that could be heard was the club music. Everyone looked at Niya to see what was going to be done, because the decision of whether or not Alexus stayed or left was totally up to her. MHB was going to back whatever the decision was, and that included Prada. Niya took one good look at Alexus, then nodded her head.

"Happy Birthday, sweety. Come take a seat right here next to me," Niya said, managing to crack a smile.

Gwen pulled up and parked two blocks away from the Food Lion on Beatties Ford Road. She was supposed to meet up with Master for a routine drug transaction. She was glad to finally see his blue Cadillac pull up and park a few cars away from hers. The heavy rain beat down on the windshield as Gwen waited for Master to get out of his car.

"I'm not coming out in that rain," Gwen said, breaking the silence in her car. Master wasn't getting out of his car either. For about two minutes, they both played the waiting game until Gwen decided to call him. She reached into the center console and grabbed her phone, along with the 10 shot 9mm Glock. Master picked up on the first ring.

"Yo, what up shawty?" Master said, inhaling the thick green smoke from his Swisher Sweet.

"You gonna get out of the car, or are you gonna make me wait here all day?" Gwen said, looking out of the driver side window at all the rain puddles in the street.

"Nah, shawty. I be wit you in a second. I just got to finish countin' my money," he answered, now exhaling the weed smoke.

Gwen just hung up the phone and tossed it back into the console. It was always some shit wit Master every time she dealt with him. Too much shit for him to only be buying one half of a brick. Minutes had passed, and the rain wasn't letting up at all. It was to the point where Gwen was about to pull off and catch up wit Master later. When a green Chevy Tahoe turned onto the street, and caught Gwen's attention, chills ran through her whole body. Something wasn't right, and she could feel it.

Master still hadn't gotten out of his car, and the SUV was slowly making its way down the street. She grabbed the Glock that was sitting on her lap and checked to make sure there was a cartridge in the chamber. The moment she started her car and put it in drive, the green truck sped up and came to a screeching halt, right beside Gwen's car. The Tahoe blocked her car in, so that she couldn't move, and then finally the side door opened.

Gwen's heart was racing. Out the corner of her eye, she could see Master getting out of his car, but she still had her main view on the truck. Gwen didn't waste another second opening fire on the SUV. Several bullets crashed out of her driver side window and into the open side door where a hooded gunman attempted to jump out. As she fired, Gwen climbed over into the passenger side, opened the door, and fell out onto the pavement.

"Get da bitch! Get her and don't kill her," Master yelled out to the occupants of the Chevy Tahoe.

Hearing that, Gwen sent two fireballs his way, forcing him to take cover behind his car. Suddenly, the driver side and passenger side doors to the truck opened. The hooded gunman came out of the side door. One attempted to come around to the passenger side of Gwen's car, but rapid gunfire stopped him in his tracks. She cupped both of her hands around the gun and squeezed. The bullet tore through his chest, then another one knocked off a nice chunk of his face. Master, along with the other two shooters watched as their fellow gunman's body dropped to the ground. The all fired heavily in Gwen's direction from all angles. It was only four shots left in her gun, and the only thing on her mind was reaching the extra clip under the driver seat.

"Fuck dat bitch, dog... we out," one of the gunmen yelled to Master as he backed up to the truck.

A momentary reprieve from gunfire gave Gwen the opportunity to get up from the ground. She fired two shots in the men's direction before reaching under her seat for the extra clip. As she popped a fresh one into her gun, the green Tahoe pulled off. She came from behind her car, firing several more shots into the back of the SUV. She continued firing, hitting the back of Master's car as he tried to pull off. The multiple bullets shattered his back window, and before he could make it to the end of the street, his car crashed into a couple of parked cars. Gwen just stepped over the dead body, jumped into her car, and reversed back down the street.

As the club winded down for the night, the heavy crowd of people began to exit the building. Niya and Prada sat at the booth, pretty much waiting for everyone else to leave before they did. Diamond on the other hand, had an after party to attend.

"Alright bitches, I'm gone for the night," Diamond announced, grabbing her bag from the VIP. "Call me in the morning," she told the girls as she hurried to leave. "Wait, wait, wait. Bitch where you goin, and why are you in a hurry?" Tiffany asked, with a curious look on her face.

"None of ya damn business, girl I'm grown," she shot back with a lustful grin.

Everyone couldn't help but to laugh at Diamond, knowing exactly where she was going. Mike had her nose wide open after the first shot of dick, and now, she just couldn't get enough. He couldn't either, because he had come down to the club to pick her up

"What's wrong wit you?" Prada asked Niya who was looking across the room at Tiki and Alexus sitting at the empty bar.

"Nothin. I just got a lot on my mind right now, girl," she said, taking a sip of her drink. "Do you know that the word on the streets is that MHB is the one who robbed Mayo's stash house," she asked.

"Who told you that"

"You know Gwen came by my house earlier, talkin about she didn't know MHB started robbing people," Niya explained with an attitude

Niya was more worried about whether or not Gwen was going to rat her out to Mayo and his boys. That would be a death sentence for Niya if she ever got caught slippin. "Well look, I think I got the last two digits to the safe, so if you still wanna make it happen, you got to let me know. I'm starting to feel uncomfortable layin' up in that house," Prada said.

The truth of the matter, was that Prada was really starting to catch feelings for Mayo. It didn't matter how she kept her guard up on him, the more time she spent with him, the more she started to see what kind of man he really was. Despite being able to blow a man's head off without thinking twice about it, Mayo was good to Prada. He took her shopping, gave her money, let her drive one of his cars, and the sex was on 100%. It was starting to become pointless to rob him when she was at the point where she could almost get anything from him. The only way she could still go through with it, was if it was done immediately.

"Go ahead and put it together,"Niya said, before getting her things and leaving.

As JR walked into the house, the aroma of weed smacked him in the face. This was very unusual, considering nobody in the house smoked weed. On point, he pulled the gun from his waist and cautiously walked through the house. The smell was coming the strongest from upstairs, so that's where JR went. He went from room to room, clearing every inch of the second floor like he was a member of the swat team. He made it to his bedroom door in a matter of seconds.

If dis bitch got a nigga up in here, I'ma kill both of them, JR thought to himself, gripping the gun in his hand a little tighter.

He opened the bathroom door and saw Gwen sitting in a tub full of water with a blunt in her mouth the size of a cigar. A bottle of Patron was also in arm's reach. JR could tell from her glassy eyes that something had happened. Instinctively, he still looked around the bathroom, then back into the bedroom, just in case a nigga wanted to pop out.

"What's goin' on baby girl?" JR asked, walking over and taking a seat on the edge of the tub.

Gwen just sat there. She didn't say a word at first. The events that took place in the last three hours were still registering in her head.

"Gwen, I can't help you if you don't tell me w—"

"They tried to kidnap me today," her slurred voice spoke. "This bitch muthafucka tried to get at me," she said, taking a puff of the marijuana.

Instead of snapping out like he started to, JR did his best to remain calm. He knew that was the only way he was going to get the answers he wanted. "Who tried to kidnap you, Gwen?" JR asked, placing his gun on top of the sink.

Gwen could hardly keep her head from submerging under water as she splashed around, juggling the blunt and the bottle of tequila. JR calmly removed the blunt and the bottle of out of her hands and placed them away from her. He then grabbed a towel, picked up Gwen's naked body from the tub, took her into the bedroom and laid her down on the bed. She just turned over and began to cry. She really wasn't in the mood to talk about it, and JR could see that. Frustrated and hurt, all he could do was wait until morning when the weed and alcohol wore off. Until that time came, he wasn't going to get a wink of sleep.

Chapter 6

A knock at the door woke Mrs. Walters up from the catnap she was taking on the couch. She hadn't seen her son in a few days, and that was unusual, especially since she had his three year old daughter there. When Mrs. Walters got to the door, she feared the worst as she looked up at Det. Butler and Det. Rose.

"Good afternoon ma'am. I was wondering if you knew someone by the name of Jeffrey David," Det. Rose spoke in a sorrowful manner.

Mrs. Walters' knees gave out, and the tears poured from her eyes like a river. Dro was her son. Her only son at that, and the detectives didn't even have to say the words for her to know that he was gone. She couldn't speak; she just dropped to her knees and cupped her face in her hands.

"Mama, what's wrong?" a young lady yelled as she ran from the kitchen. "What happened? What's going on?" the girl asked the detectives while she got down and comforted her mother.

"Myyy baaabyyy ..." Mrs. Walters cried out.

"I'm sorry, but do you know this man?" Det. Butler asked the young lady, passing her Dro's ID.

"Yeah, that's my brother," she responded, looking at the driver's license. "What happened?"

"I'm sorry ma'am, but we found his body..."

The detective couldn't finish his sentence, as both women cried out. It hurt Det. Rose so much that she had to turn her head. This was the hardest part of her job, telling someone that a loved-one had been murdered. Butler felt the same way, but his skin was a little tougher.

Gwen's head was pounding before she could even open her eyes. Everything was fuzzy except for the events that took place last night. She rolled over to see JR sitting in a chair next to the bed, with his gun on his lap, looking right at her. He didn't get a moment of rest all night. How could he? He came home to find his girl pissy drunk, talking about somebody tried to kidnap her.

"Wha... what time is it?" Gwen asked, trying to clear her throat.

"It's 11:00," JR answered, passing Gwen a cup of water and two pills for the headache he knew she had.

The bruise on the side of her face was throbbing. It must have happened when Gwen climbed out of the passenger side door and fell to the pavement. JR had to look at that bruise all night, which made him furious.

"Now Gwen, I want you to tell me everything that happened last night, and I don't want you to leave out a single detail," JR demanded in an aggressive manner.

The aggression wasn't towards her, but rather towards the nigga who tried to take her. Through the grogginess in her voice, she began to tell JR what happened. The more she talked, the more he couldn't believe what he was hearing.

Master must have lost his fucking mind, he thought to himself as Gwen told the story.

He knew Master pretty well, and Master knew him. That was the confusing part about it. Master knew JR didn't play any games, and wouldn't hesitate to put a bullet in a nigga's head for fucking with his girl.

"Mike, my man," Mayo spoke as he opened his front door.

"Mayo, it's good to see you," Mike said, shaking Mayo's hand before entering the house.

Besides being probably the biggest drug dealer in Charlotte right now, Mayo had his hands in the real estate game. He bought houses and land all over Charlotte, and made a killing reselling or renting the properties out. Before Mike, it was hard for him to sell anything. Mike changed all that and made real estate profitable for Mayo.

"I got some good news for you. I sold the lot on Point Breeze last night, the bank should be transferring the money into your account sometime today," Mike told Mayo.

"See, that's why I fuck wit you, Mike. I don't have to tell you how to do your job like other people I work with," Mayo said, putting his arm around Mike's shoulder and walking him into the kitchen.

"Hey, make Mike a plate," he directed Prada who was already in the process of cooking.

Mike looked over to see who Mayo was referring to, and noticed Prada. At first, he couldn't figure out where he knew her from, and then it hit him. He remembered her from the club the other night. She was with Diamond when he went to pick her up. Prada noticed him too, but didn't say anything. She hoped Mike didn't say anything either and cause Mayo to start probing.

The relationship between Mike and Mayo had grown over the months until it became more than just business. They were somewhat friends. Mike was a white man, but he acted just like a black man. That's one of the reasons Diamond was feeling him the way she was. He had swag, most of which came from being around Mayo.

"We gotta celebrate, Mike, let's hit the club tonight," Mayo suggested.

"Not tonight, Mayo. I got a date already," he said, thinking about the plans he and Diamond had for the night.

"Well, it's me and you this weekend, Mike, and I'm not taking no for an answer," Mayo joked.

Mike, Mayo, and Prada sat at the table and ate their breakfast, talking and just joking around for the rest of the morning. It was a little awkward at the table for Mike and Prada, and at times, Mayo caught on to it, but didn't say anything.

Niya got out of the shower and headed downstairs for breakfast. When she got there, it was something other than breakfast waiting at the table. Niya almost had a heart attack when she saw her whole stash sitting on the table. Chad even had the twin Glock .40 cals, a .380, a .45 cal, and the AR-15 sitting next to the stacks of money. Chad stood off to the side, just staring at Niya with a blank look on his face. It was so quiet in the house, Niya didn't even notice that the twins weren't home. Chad made sure he dropped them off at daycare, so they wouldn't hear the arguing.

"So you're going through my stuff now, Chad?" Niya said, breaking the silence.

"Goin through ya stuff? Last time I checked, this was my

muthafuckin' house," Chad barked back. "What da fuck is you out here doin'?"

"Nothin' Chad!"

"Nothin' Chad? What do you think, I'm a fuckin fool? Where the fuck is you getting all this money from?"

The first thing that came to his mind, just like any other man, was that she was stepping out on him. It was too much money to think otherwise, not to mention the fact that she had guns in the stash too.

"Ni, I'm not gonna keep fuckin asking you. Who fuckin money and guns are these?" he said, walking towards her.

He was trying to get into striking range, because he was about two seconds away from smacking the shit out of her. She felt it too, and moved from one side of the kitchen table to the other. Even though Chad was trying to be a different person, Niya knew that he still had that killer in him, and was not to be played with.

"It's mine, Chad. The money and the guns. It's all mine," she said, looking down at the table.

Chad inched his way closer. He knew that she wasn't lying. Not one time did he ever put his hands on Niya during their whole relationship, but today he was on the brink.

"Look how we're livin' Chad," Niya started to explain. "You live paycheck to paycheck, Chad, and don't get me wrong, I respect you for that. But you deserve to have... don't we deserve to have more?"

"I live paycheck to paycheck because I have to, Niya," C yelled in frustration. "I decided to leave the streets alone reason and one reason only, and that was for the sake of y kids. Now here you are telling me I ain't shit; that I'm for my wife and kids. Really Ni, that's what you saying to me? That my woman has to step up for me?"

Chad wasn't a slouch by a long shot, and his retirement from the street made it possible for nigga's like Mayo to eat. There weren't too many people in the history of Charlotte, North Carolina who had done it as big as him. It wasn't until he got shot, and indicted by the feds that he realized the more important things in life, like family. The feds pretty much took everything he had. He beat the case, but the feds wasn't gonna give him back the money that they knew came from drugs. That's when life started to become less luxurious for him.

"Chad, don't do that," Niya said, starting to feel the effects of what he was saying.

"Don't do what? You think I like dis shit. You think I don't miss the money? I work every fucking day so that I can come home to you every night, but I guess that's not good enough!" he yelled. "Now, where did you get this fuckin money," he screamed, smacking the stack of money off the table.

He moved closer, but when he did, Niya did something she would later regret. It may have been out of fear, or just a spur of the moment type of situation, but she looked down at the .40 caliber that was still on the table, and flinched as if she was about to grab it. She snatched her hand back, but the damage was done. Chad had seen her reaction. He just looked at her. The anger in him drifted away, but was replaced by sadness. Niya could see the hurt written all over his face and the moisture it brought to his eyes.

"Oh yeah, you was..."

"No boo, I'm sorry," Niya pleaded, trying to walk up to him.

He grabbed her by the throat when she got close enough, and st pushed her away. The thought of grabbing one of the guns off table and blowing her head off crossed his mind, but he decided against it. He just stepped over the money and walked out the kitchen. His heart was crushed more than anything, and Niya knew it. She knew she had fucked up, and there was nothing she could do about it.

Master lay on his side, going in and out of consciousness when Det. Rose and Det. Butler walked into his room. Despite the couple of family members sitting in the room, they did what they do best, and started asking questions.

"Mr. Miller, do you know who shot you?" Butler asked repeatedly every time Master's eyes would open.

The bullet had caused some damage when it entered his back. It was still stuck inside of him, and the doctors weren't too optimistic about removing it, because it was resting against his spine. One wrong move and the bullet could paralyze him. Gwen wasn't even aware that she had hit him. She saw him crash, but didn't stick around to find out why.

"Can you leave him alone?" one of the women sitting in the room asked the detectives.

"Ma'am, we need to find out who did this," Det. Rose responded while Butler continued to question Master.

Both detectives knew that they had a short window to work with in finding the shooter, and now would be the best time to question the victim. Morphine mixed with pain added up to the strong possibility of a confession. The chances of Master telling them who shot him were better now than if he were fully conscious. The detectives just hoped that he would slip up and give them a name.

Chapter 7

"Yo, hurry up in there... We're gonna be late fuckin around wit you," Mayo yelled out to Prada who was still in the bathroom.

Prada had managed to get some Kevin Hart tickets at the last minute, and persuaded Mayo to take her to the comedy show. It was grown and sexy night, so Mayo had on a brown and blue cardigan with a polo button-up underneath, a pair of dark blue Diesel slacks and Gucci loafers. On his wrist was a Rolex. He tried to keep it basic for the night, considering after the show, it was the after party.

"I'm coming, I'm coming," Prada grumbled, coming out of the bathroom.

"Dam!" Mayo said out loud, looking over at her.

Prada had on all white and a pair of gold Louis Vuitton heels. She was stunning. This was the reason why she had made it this far with Mayo.

"You better be on ya best behavior tonight, or you'll miss out on dessert," she teased in a seductive manner. "I know it's gonna be a lot of bitches there, so let me give you something to think about before we leave this house," Prada said, walking over to Mayo who was sitting on the bed.

She dropped to her knees, right between his legs, unfastened his pants, and pulled them down to his ankles. Mayo sat back on his elbows and watched as Prada took him into her mouth. She slowly swallowed every bit of nine inches of meat, causing Mayo's toes to curl in his loafers. The warm, wet spit could be felt running down his balls as Prada continued to suck. Her head bobbed up and down, going faster and faster, the more she got into it. She periodically took it out of her mouth so that she could French kiss the top of it. She looked up at him so she could see the look on his face while she performed.

Mayo was at the point where he could feel himself about to cum. He tried to grab her by the back of her hair and pull her off of him, but Prada just kept sucking and sucking. He even tried to get up, but she pushed him back on the bed. He was about to cum and she could feel it.

"Shit!" he yelled out, now resting both of his hands on her head. He started pushing her head up and down on his dick until he couldn't hold it anymore. He exploded inside of her mouth with force.

"Aahhhh," he yelled as he could feel his warm cum on her tongue.

Prada didn't waste a drop, she swallowed everything. She continued to suck on it for another minute or two, just to make sure it was gone.

"They're just now leaving the house," Niya said, getting back into the car with Alexus.

Niya and Alexus had been parked around the corner from Mayo's house for the past two hours, waiting for Prada to get him out. Tonight was the night for them to move on Mayo's safe. The only thing that really bothered Niya, was the fact that she had to bring Alexus along for the move. Diamond was nowhere to be found, and Tiffany was at the hospital with her Mom, so the only person left to accompany Niya, was Alexus.

"Now, no matter what, don't get out of this car," Niya told Alexus while putting on latex gloves.

Prada had provided Niya with everything. The house key, the alarm code, and the safe's six-digit code, was all she needed. It was as if she lived there, the way she calmly let herself into the house and disarmed the security system.

Mayo's house was huge. It was like a mini mansion, and for a second, Niya stopped to admire his house design. Large comfortable sofas, beautiful paintings on the wall, a piano, and a large bearskin rug rested in front of a stone fireplace. All this, and Niya wasn't even out of the living room.

"You know, the only thing better than love, is loyalty. That's what a good friend of mine told me," Mayo said, breaking the silence in the car. "Do you know anything about loyalty?" he asked Prada, cutting his eyes at her for a brief second before looking back at the road ahead of him.

The question came from out of nowhere, and it confused Prada for a second. She didn't know how to respond to that, or even if he really wanted her to. She had to sit and think about the answer she was about to give, but right before she could say anything, Mayo's Blackberry started to chirp. He grabbed it out of the center console and looked at the text message that was just sent to him.

"What? You forget that you was supposed to take ya other girlfriend out today?" Prada joked, pushing the top of his shoulder.

He just looked at her and smiled. They were halfway downtown when Mayo announced that he needed to make a quick stop before the show.

"Business," he told her as he pulled off the highway.

"Now... come on boo, we're gonna be late," Prada pleaded, hoping to keep him on course.

"I can't miss out on this one babe, but I promise you we'll make it to the show on time," Mayo assured.

Prada didn't care about the show. She really just wanted to make sure Mayo didn't intend to go back to the house. If he did, he would be walking right in on Niya. That was something Prada knew neither Niya nor her could afford. Not only would he kill her, he would most likely put two and two together, and find out that Prada had something to do with it, and kill her too. All Prada could do was sit back and hope that wasn't the case.

Niya looked up the long row of stairs, skeptical about going up. It was dark as hell, and to be honest, she was a little scared. She pulled the compact black on black, .45 off her waist, thinking to herself that she had come too far to turn around now. She proceeded up the stairs with caution, cupping the gun in both hands and praying that there was no one in the house. Ironically, she was more scared that a ghost would jump out from somewhere, instead of a human. It got so bad, that she started to turn on every light switch she passed. Once she got to the room where the safe was, she became a little more relaxed, tucking her gun into her back pocket and pulling out the small piece of paper with the safe's code on it. She immediately started punching numbers into the small box on the outside of the door, but the safe wasn't opening.

"2...5...1...1," she mumbled to herself as she kept trying to punch the code in. "Damn, Prada," she mumbled, becoming frustrated.

She remembered Prada saying that she couldn't get the last

number, but thought that it was the number one. With that, Niya began punching in the code, but changing the last digit every time one wouldn't work. "Yessssss!" she yelled after pushing 251167 into the keypad, and the door unlocked.

When she opened the door, her eyes opened wide as fifty cent pieces. She had never seen so much money, guns, and drugs in her life. Prada wasn't lying when she said Mayo had a safe. She looked at the small duffle bag she brought with her, and knew for sure that she was going to need something bigger to carry this stuff out. Niya thought that she might have had to make two trips to haul everything out.

When she turned around to see if she could find a trash bag in the house, a blow connected to her face, which felt like she had been hit with a sledgehammer. The impact of JR's fist to the right side of her face caused Niya to fall back into the safe, knocking stuff off the shelves on her way to the ground. JR grabbed her by the ankle and dragged her out of the safe. Niya was knocked out cold, but JR woke her up with several body shots.

"You dumb bitch. You really thought you was gonna pull this off?" JR said, standing over her. He then pulled a large .357 revolver out of his waist and pointed it at Niya's head.

She was still dazed, and couldn't see very well, but she could hear the hammer cocking back very clearly. Chad and the twins were the only things that crossed her mind. She knew that it was her time to die, and before she did, she began to pray to herself.

Mayo pulled over into a rest stop right off the highway. Prada didn't have any problem with that, as long as he wasn't going back home. She was hoping that Niya and Alexus were handling their business, because she was so ready for this situation to be over. Not wanting to show her stress, she just looked out the window at the large eighteen-wheelers coming and leaving the rest stop.

"You know something that's crazy," Mayo began, "I really like you Prada. You got a lot goin for yourself and I can see the great potential in you. I just hope everything works out," he said, looking down at his phone as though he was waiting for a call or text.

"I like you too, May, but why are you talking like this?" Prada asked with a confused look on her face. Had he picked up on my vibe? She wondered to herself.

Mayo continued, "All my life, I've learned that it's the people closest to you that will hurt you the most. I'm just hoping you're not one of them," he said, looking her in her eyes with a stern look.

Now he was making Prada nervous. He was starting to talk crazy, and Prada also noticed the change in his body language ever since he got the text earlier. Nervousness quickly turned into fear and before she knew it, Prada was looking for an exit strategy. Looking outside of her window she noticed that she really didn't have anywhere to go. Her best chance was a gas station that looked like it was about a quarter of a mile away. Mayo's phone ringing snapped her out of her thoughts.

"Yo, what's good, homie?" Mayo answered, looking over at Prada who was looking back out the window.

"Yeah, you were right, bro. Shawty here right now wit her hand in the cookie jar," JR said, looking down at a groggy Niya.

"Oh yeah?"

"Yeah, and she got a MHB tattoo on her wrist," JR told him. "So what you wanna do?"

"You already know, homie. Take care of dat and get rid of the body," Mayo instructed, and then hung up the phone. "Can you believe somebody broke into my house and tried to rob me?" Mayo said, turning his attention to Prada. "A bitch at that," he chuckled.

Prada's heart started racing uncontrollably, and the only thing she wanted to do at that moment, was get out of the car, which she knew Mayo wouldn't allow. A vision of Niya being executed like Dro was, flashed through her mind. Just the thought of losing her best friend brought tears to her eyes.

"Don't cry, sweetie, Yeah, I know it hurt, shawty. She's as good as dead," Mayo taunted, having put two and two together in a matter of seconds.

"I'm sorry, May," Prada cried, knowing she'd been caught.

Tears fell down her face, but Mayo didn't pay the tears any mind. Prada reached for her bag as if she was looking for some tissue to clean her face off. While she reached for her bag, Mayo was reaching for his gun that was located in the side panel of the driver side door. Inside of her bag, Prada felt around, but it wasn't for tissue. Her hand locked onto the baby .380 auto that lived there. This was her only chance. It was do or die. As she began to pull her hand out of her bag, Mayo was pulling the gun from the side of his door.

It all came down to who was the quickest on the draw, and for Mayo, he saw Prada's stunt a mile away. She never got the chance to pull it out, as a single shot from his gun flashed before her eyes. The bullet entered the center of her forehead and never exited, killing her instantly. Mayo was glad he had invested in the hollow tip bullets, that way, he didn't have to worry about the splatter of blood and tissue from the bullet wound. He got out of the car and walked around to the passenger side. He looked around a few times to make sure nobody saw what happened, before pulling her body out of the car and tossing it to the ground like Prada was a piece of trash. He looked at her once more, and shook his head in disappointment at her betrayal. The love he was starting to develop for her all but disappeared with the confirmation call he had received from JR. To

Mayo, Prada was just like any other trick or nigga that had ever crossed him.

JR tucked his cell phone in his pocket, and then looked down at Niya. He leaned over and pointed the .357 at her head. Finally getting her bearings, Niya looked up at the man who was about to take her life. "See you in the next life, shawty," JR said.

He put his finger on the trigger, and was about to squeeze, when out of nowhere he heard a gun cocking back. He turned around to see Alexus standing there with a gun in her hand, pointing it right at him. He attempted to fire, but Alexus didn't hesitate. She began firing round after round into JR's direction. What she lacked in accuracy she made up for with numbers. JR managed to get off two shots in the midst of Alexus raining bullets on him, but neither one hit her.

It was the last two bullets that Alexus fired that made contact with JR. One in his leg and the other one tore through his gut. He dropped to one knee, but still had his gun in his hand. Seeing that Alexus was out of bullets and JR was still moving, Niya reached for the .45 in her back pocket, popped the safety off and began firing at JR before he could raise his gun again at Alexus.

Pow! Pow! Pow! One bullet hit him in the side of his face, and another hit his neck, splitting open his jugular. Blood shot out of his neck like a faucet, and he was dead before he fell the rest of the way to the ground. Niya got to her feet, gun in hand and still pointed at JR. She made sure he was dead, then unarmed him before running over to the bed and pulling the sheet off of it.

"Lex, get over here," Niya yelled out. "Help me get dis shit out of here," she said, laying the sheet out on the floor in front of the safe.

She definitely didn't have time to be making two trips, especially knowing that Mayo and Prada was more than likely on their way back to the house. As fast as they could move, Alexus and Niya loaded everything of value into the sheet, wrapped it up as tightly as they could, then left the house.

Mayo pulled into his driveway and saw that the front door was wide open. A lot of lights were on in the house as well, which made him proceed with extreme caution. He pulled the 9mm from his waist, then entered the home. It was quiet, and he still wasn't sure if it was safe or not.

"Yo homie," Mayo yelled out, seeing if JR was gonna respond.

There was no answer. Mayo continued up the stairs until he reached the room where the safe was located. He could now see why he wasn't getting an answer from JR. His friend was laying in a pool of blood, dead with his eyes open. Frustrated, hurt, and mad as hell, Mayo walked over and looked into his safe. It was pretty much empty except for the jewelry Niya had left behind. He walked back over to JR's body and kneeled down next to it. Mayo placed his hand over his dead partner's eyes and wiped them close. He shook his head in disbelief at the outcome of his plan. This bitch, Niya, had not only robbed him again, but now she had taken the life of someone he really cared about. He took a huge gasp before speaking out loud to his deceased childhood friend.

"Damn homie. I'ma hold you down family, that's my word. All these bitches gonna pay, my nigga, I put that on everythang." Mayo said, resting the gun on the side of his head.

Part II

Chapter 1

Security was a little tight in the emergency room, due to the rash of violence in Charlotte over the past night. Cops were everywhere, but that didn't stop Gwen from entering the hospital with one thing on her mind, and that was to find out why Master had tried to kidnap her. She had gotten word through some street connections, that he was now housed up in the ICU at Carolina Medical Center. The thought of that nigga still breathing wasn't sitting right with her, and despite JR promising he was going to take care of it, she wasn't in the mood for waiting. A large pair of Gucci frames covered a nice portion of Gwen's face. That along with a full-length blonde wig, made the perfect disguise for her in the event Master forced her to do more than question him, at that time. Instead of bringing her gun into the hospital, Gwen brought her trusty butterfly knife, so that if she did decide to kill him, it would be quiet.

After getting Master's room number from the nurse at the front desk, Gwen proceeded to the 4th floor where he was at. The whole time walking down the hall, Gwen played back in her mind that day when they came after her. It made her more and more furious, just thinking about it. She looked up at every room number she passed by, until she finally came upon the number the nurse had given her.

"422," she mumbled to herself, looking into the room to see Master lying in the bed with all kinds of needles and tubes sticking out of him.

"Who are you?" a young female asked, startling Gwen.

It was Master's sister sitting in the chair off to the side. Gwen hadn't noticed her upon entering the room, and was startled. She was also pissed at the fact that Master wasn't alone. She managed to fake a smile, and answer the curious young women's question.

"Hi, I'm a friend of Master's," Gwen lied, thinking fast. "I just stopped by to see how he was doing."

Master's sister wasn't too alarmed. She just figured that Gwen was another one of Master's girlfriends who was checking in on him. "Well, he's doin' a lot better. The doctor said that he should make a full recovery. He just needs to get his rest," she informed Gwen.

Gwen looked over at Master, mad as hell after hearing he was going to be alright. Master's sister didn't think nothing of it when Gwen walked over and stood by his bedside. She looked down on him, placed her hand on his side a few inches away from his bullet wound and squeezed. It wasn't enough morphine in his system that could stop him from feeling that. His eyes shot wide open, the heart monitor started beeping fast, and the bullet wound in his back started to bleed. "He must be happy to see me," Gwen looked over and told his sister to try to take her attention off the suddenly rapid beeping noise from the monitor.

Master's sister simply dug her face back into the hair magazine she was reading. Gwen turned her attention back to Master, who was still somewhat in shock. She leaned in, as though she was kissing the side of his face, in order to talk without being heard by his sister.

"Why?" she whispered in his ear as she held a firm grip to his side.

The pain mixed with a dry throat made it hard for him to speak. He was trying to say something, but Gwen couldn't really hear him through the oxygen mask. She pulled the mask down from his face, but the moment she did, the heart monitor started going crazy. It was too loud for Master's sister to ignore. Not only his sister, but also a nurse came rushing to his bedside. Gwen just backed up and let the two women attend to him.

"What happened?" both women asked her simultaneously.

"I don't know, I just gave him a kiss on the cheek and he woke up, I think he pulled his mask off to say something to me."

While the nurse and Master's sister focused back on Master, Gwen quickly disappeared from the room.

Detective Rose and Detective Butler pushed through the early morning traffic to arrive at the Pilot rest stop off highway I-85. When they pulled up, they were greeted by the patrol officer who was first on the scene. He walked them over to where Prada's blood soaked body was, right next to an 18-wheeler. Off the top, Butler could see the cause of death was a bullet wound to the head.

"She's too well put together to be a hooker," Det. Rose said as she analyzed the body.

"Whoa, we got a gun," Butler said, looking into Prada's Louie bag that was off to the side.

Butler looked deeper into her bag and found her I.D., along with some cash. From that, he quickly ruled out the possibility of a robbery.

"We got a witness too," the patrol officer announced, grabbing both Rose and Butler's attention.

You could see the excitement in both of their eyes. Homicides were the toughest cases to prove in the criminal justice system, without the proper evidence. Anyone who had ever viewed an episode of The First 48 understood that. But when there was a witness, an eye witness to the crime, it's like a blessing from God for homicide detectives. The patrol officer walked the two detectives around to the other side of the 18-wheeler, where John, the truck driver sat. John retold them the story of how he was asleep in his truck when he was awakened by a pop. He didn't think much of it, considering where he was, but curiosity made him take a peek out his window. That's when he saw a man pulling the body of a female out of his car.

He said that he didn't get a real good look at the man, however he was sure he was African-American. He also was certain that the car was a Mercedes Benz S550, all black. Because the car turned around so quickly, he didn't get a chance to see the rear license plate. But he had seen the front vanity plate clearly. He remembered trying to figure out why someone would put the name of some mayonnaise on the front of such a beautiful and expensive car.

"The tag read, Mayo," He repeated to both detectives again.

Rose asked if he would be able to identify the man who was driving the car if he was to see him again. John said that he was not sure, but he would try. Even though it was a small lead, it was a break in the investigation, and it had been in less than thirty minutes of the detectives being on the case. Now came the hard part, and that was having to make the trip to the victim's family's home to give them the sad news of their loss. Both officers dreaded this part of the job the most.

Gwen wisely had left the hospital after drawing all the attention to Master's room. She was just gonna have to wait until he was a little better before confronting the situation again. She headed back home with somewhat of a bitter taste in her mouth. When she finally did make it home, it was the line of older cars with 24 inch rims sitting out front of her apartment building that caught her attention first. This wasn't the kind of complex were the occupants drove those types of vehicles. Gwen became more concerned when she could hear the sounds of men laughing and joking coming from the inside of her front door. Pressing her ear to the door she could hear the faint voices of men inside of her apartment. She looked up and down the hall, not sure as to what she should do because she had no idea what was on the other side of the entry. Before she had a chance to react, the apartment door swung open and a short, stocky, black man stood before her with the grimiest look on his face. The look alone scared the shit out of her.

"Yo... come on in shawty," the man said, stepping to the side so that she could enter.

Gwen looked at him like he was crazy. Before he got a chance to say another word, Gwen took a step back, dropped her pocketbook, and pulled the 9mm from out of her back waist. It happened so fast, the guy at the door didn't have time to do anything but put his hands in the air.

"Who da fuck are you, and what you doin' in my apartment?" Gwen shouted, hoping to get her next door neighbor's attention.

"Whoa... Whoa... Whoa..." Mayo yelled as he ran to the door. "Gwen, it's me," he said hoping it would calm her down.

Gwen began to somewhat lower the gun, after seeing a familiar face. But she was still cautiously hugging the trigger of the firearm. "And who da fuck is you, acting like I suppose to know your ass." she asked, still pointing the gun at the first guy.

"I'm Roni, a friend of JR's. Remember I met you at his Mom's house when she had the Thanksgiving dinner last year?" he explained.

Gwen was still on edge with the whole kidnapping situation, so she eased up a little bit, but was still watchful.

"Why are ya'll in my apartment?" she asked, lowering the gun all the way, now, but still keeping it in her hand. "And where the fuck is JR?"

Mayo lowered his head, preparing to give Gwen the sad news. He still had the memory of seeing JR's dead body in his house. When he did that, Gwen knew that it wasn't good news. She poked her head further into the apartment, and could see a couple more guys sitting on her couch with sad looks on their faces.

"JR was murdered last night, shawty," Mayo said in a low tone with a quiver in his voice.

It was like somebody had taken a knife, and stabbing her directly in the heart when she heard those words. She backed up until her back hit the living room wall. She slid down it until she was sitting on the floor. She couldn't even stand up anymore, and the more and more it registered in her head, the more she cried. JR had always been there for her, and even though she never could love him as much as he had loved her, there was a special bond between them.

Niya woke up to see Jasmine playing with one of her toys in the living room. Niya was still in the dog house with Chad, so the couch had become her new best friend. At this point, it wasn't clear where her and Chad's relationship stood, but the one thing she knew, was that she didn't want to lose him. In her heart, she felt guilty because she knew the sacrifices he made by getting out of the game, and she knew that those sacrifices was the best thing for their family.

"Jazzy Pooh," Niya said, calling Jasmine by her nickname. "Where's ya bro bro?" she asked looking around the room for Jahmil.

"Heee... up dere," baby Jasmine said, pointing up.

Niya's ringing cell phone interrupted the short mother, daughter time they were having. She ran to get it, hoping it was Prada finally returning her many calls. She was waiting to hear how Mayo was taking the loss of the contents of his safe. Niya didn't even look at the screen, she just hit accept and began talking.

"Damn bitch, it took you long enough to return my calls. That nigga must have been crying all night on your shoulders," Niya spoke with a little chuckle.

"Ni it's D," Diamond uttered in a low tone.

"Oh, what up D? I thought you were Prada." Niya answered, sitting back on the couch.

The phone went silent for a second, and then all Niya could hear was Diamond crying on the other end.

"D, what's wrong?" Niya asked. "Talk to me Diamond, what's going on?" Niya pleaded through Diamond's cries.

"Sheeesss gone, Ni," Diamond cried out. "He... killed... her," she managed to get out.

"Who, Diamond? Who got killed?" Niya asked frantically.

It was a moment of silence on the phone. In that moment, a million and one thoughts ran through Niya's mind. She knew who Diamond was talking about, but nothing inside of her wanted to believe it. She began shaking her head from left to right as her eyes filled up with tears.

"No, I don't believe you. You lying, Diamond!"

"Prada is dead, Ni!"

"Diamond you take that shit back. Don't you play like that!"

"They killed her, Ni," Diamond cried out, this time even louder.

Niya dropped the phone and fell to the floor. It was as if hearing the words collapsed her heart. There wasn't a single term in the dictionary that could describe how she felt, not only to have lost a friend who was like a blood sister, but to know that she was the cause. She knew she should have gotten Prada out of harm's way, earlier. Her stomach began to knot up, and the tears poured out of Niya's eyes. Baby Jasmine began crying, matching her mother's screams.

All the noise brought Chad running down the steps to see what was going on. When he arrived and saw the two most important women of his life on the floor wailing their eyes out, he went over and picked up Jasmine in one arm, and pulled Niya close to him with the other.

"Ni, what's the matter?" He asked, trying to calm her down, so he could understand her words.

"Prada is dead, they killed my best friend... I killed my best friend!" Niya shouted out.

Chad didn't ask any more questions. He had lost enough friends in the street to know now wasn't the time. He just pulled Niya closer to him and held his two girls in his arms, like he never wanted to let go.

Detective Rose sat at her desk searching the police data-base for the alias name of "Mayo". She wasn't having much luck. That was until another officer suggested she try the domestic violent crime record.

"You know the ladies are always down here taking out restraining orders on these guys, and they always seem to list every alias or nickname they know." The young beat cop spoke.

She logged out of one search engine, and into the domestic crimes search. Rose typed in the name Mayo, and a huge smile came across her face when she saw the name "Marquis Harper" pop up on the screen with a photo beside it. She then immediately cross-referenced his name with the DMV records, and her smile got even larger. She instantly picked up the phone and called her partner, Detective Butler.

"Hey, guess who I just found? And guess what kind of car he has registered in his name? Yep, a black s550 Mercedes Benz." She spat out before Butler was able to answer one of the questions.

"That's great! Text me his address, and I will meet you over there." Butler added.

Thirty minutes later, Rose pulled up to Mayo's house. Her partner, Butler, had already arrived and was across the street at one of Mayo's neighbor's homes. He came walking back over as Rose got out of the car.

"Well, we may have something. The owner of that house, a Mr. Carey, said he heard shots being fired from inside Mr. Harper's house last night. He also said that he saw Mr. Harper and his girlfriend leave last night, not too long before he heard the shots," Butler explained.

Rose was about to go up to Mayo's door and knock to see if he was home, but Butler stopped her "I'm not done, lastly Mr. Carey said Mr. Harper returned in the wee hours of the morning and the girlfriend was not with him. The neighbor also said he left back out about two hours ago.

"Damn, so the neighbor saw all of this?" Rose asked Butler, with a curious look on his face.

"Yep!"

“Thank God for nosey neighbors.” Rose said with a laugh.

“Yeah, thank God,” Butler added while nodding in the direction of the house across the street with an old, white man sitting on his porch.

Chapter 2

The number of people that showed up to the church was in the hundreds, all to see off a good friend and great person, Kiara Monique Thompson, also known as Prada. Prada's grandmother was so surprised, she didn't even know that her granddaughter knew so many people. Prada had touched a lot of people during her time on earth, and it was a known fact that the people who loved her, outweighed the few enemies she had made. It showed, because not only was everyone from Charlotte there, it wasn't a set of dry eyes in the building. All that could be heard echoing in the church were expressions of grief.

The small church which usually held 500-600 members and guest on Sundays. Was bursting at the seams. The older, light complected pastor stood up and requested for everyone to turn to the book of John 14 & 10. His voice was so low, that the usher's had to ask the people whispering to quiet down. That didn't last long, because it seemed that the more he spoke, the louder his voice became. Pastor Culbertson was no longer speaking the words, rather singing them. He began to talk about everyone having to get prepared for their day.

"Don't you cry for Sister Thompson, she's in a better place! You better be worried about yourself, because everyone of us is going to have to follow Kiara. He continuously taught.

"Her Grandmother told me just a couple of weeks ago, that Kiara told her that she was coming back to church. She knew she had to get her life together with God again, and I know she made it right with Jesus before he called her home." All the church ushers and elders, who had seen Prada grow up, bore witness to the pastor's statement.

Even Niya felt some comfort from the words of the minister. Her and the girls were actually holding their emotions together quite well. That was until pastor Culbertson, turned and requested the choir to sing a song. The elderly choir director stood up first, then motioned for the rest of the choir to stand. They did as they were instructed, and began to slowly and soulfully sing.

Never would have made it, never could have made it, without you.
I would have lost it all, but now I see how you were there for me

And I can say.
Never would have made it,
Never could have made it,
Without you.

I would have lost it all,
But now I see how you were there for me, and I can say…
I'm stronger, I'm wiser, I'm better,
Much better,

When I look back over all you brought me thru.
I can see that you were the one that I held on to.

I would have lost my mind a long time ago, if it had not been for you.
I am stronger
I am wiser
Now I am better
So much better

The old man's voice was deep, but very well-toned. The pain of his years of living, and the firsthand knowledge of the words he was singing poured out through his voice. Diamond was the first to break. She let out a yell so loud, and it forced all the ushers to come running to her aid. It was good that more than one responded because Tiffany was the next to go. and it was taking three women and one man to hold Diamond. Niya's legs where shaking, and Chad could see that she was about to lose it. So he grabbed Jahmil out of her arms, and handed him to a lady sitting behind them. He did it just in the nick of time, because Niya totally lost it. She ran up to the casket, just as the funeral director was attempting to close it.

"Prada!" she yelled. "Prada please, I love you sis. I love you... Get up Prada... Please... Please... God please..." Prada's grandmother and Chad came up to get her.

They were having a difficult time, because Niya was fighting them off, but finally her body went limp. Chad was trying to hold her up, and Mrs. Thompson wasn't being much help. Chad could feel the presence of somebody walking up and standing right next to them. He looked over and couldn't believe that it was Gwen standing there with a t-shirt on that had a picture of Prada on the front with the letters RIP over her image. On the back it had the letters MHB -4-Life, she also had on some black jeans and a pair of white AirMax. She looked so hood, but so good in the way she was representing a fallen comrade.

She went over and motioned for Mrs. Thompson to let her help. She grabbed the other side of Niya. The whole time she stood there helping to hold Niya, she didn't say a word. The pastor continued by asking the pallbearers to come forward. The men grabbed the casket and escorted it out to the awaiting car.

After the body had been carried out, Prada's grandmother thought that it was best for the girls not to go to the gravesite. No one argued, and Niya found herself in the church's bathroom with her face in the sink. She picked her head up from the sink after splashing water in her face, just in time to see Gwen walking through the door.

"What the hell happened to Prada? This shit got ya name written all over it," Gwen said, leaning against the stall.

Niya's sorrow quickly turned into anger, and the tension in the room became thick in a matter of seconds.

"Now is not the time for the dumb shit, Gwen," Niya replied with an attitude, drying her face off.

Gwen thought that it wasn't a better time than today. She had some shit she wanted to get off her chest, and had been wanting to for quite some time now. The deaths of JR and Prada, and the fact that she knew Niya had something to do with it, was pretty much the breaking point.

"I'ma ask you one time... and I swear it's only going to be one time," Gwen said turning around and locking the bathroom door. "Did you have something to do with this?" She asked with a dead serious look on her face.

"I think ya best bet is to move from in front of that door and mind ya fuckin' business," Niya said as she attempted to walk towards the door.

The confrontation went from zero to sixty in a snap of a finger, when Niya reached over Gwen to unlock the door. Gwen just took off, punching Niya in her mouth. Niya's reaction time was on point as she returned the blows. It was an all-out fight. Gwen grabbed a handful of Niya's hair with her left hand, and was punching her in her gut with the right. Gwen was landing punch after punch. She had an advantage, because of the way she was dressed in sneakers and jeans. She had come ready to fight.

Right when it looked like Gwen was getting the best of Niya, the tables turned. Once Niya got out of her heels, instead of fighting against Gwen and pulling her hair, she stepped into it. She took her thumbs and jammed them into Gwen's eyes.

Ahhh... Bitch! Gwen yelled out, letting Niya's hair go.

Right, left, right, left, right, left. Niya was whaling on Gwen, who could barely see. Gwen kept on punching too. They stood toe to toe going blow for blow for a good sixty seconds.

"Let me go check on Niya," Tiffany mumbled to Diamond.

When she got downstairs in the basement where the bathroom was at, she could hear the thumping and yelling before she got there. When she finally did turn the corner, Tiki was standing outside the bathroom door eating sunflower seeds. She had seen when both Niya and Gwen left from upstairs, and was going to take the opportunity to talk to both of them together, but when she got downstairs they were already fighting.

"Just let it happen," Tiki told Tiffany when she walked up. "It's better if they get it out of their system now then later."

Tiffany couldn't do nothing but respect the veteran call. They both just stood by the door and waited for the fight to end. For females, Niya and Gwen had a lot of wind. They had been fighting and wrestling for over ten minutes straight. But the fatigue started to settle in, and the punches became slower until the point where neither of them could throw another blow. They finally broke, falling to the floor on opposite sides of the bathroom.

Niya was the first to get to her feet, stumbling to the door and unlocking it. She was shocked and somewhat embarrassed when she opened the door and saw Tiki and Tiffany standing there. Tiki just shook her head.

"Yall done with that bullshit? she asked. "Well clean up and get back upstairs." She instructed the two women before turning around, grabbing Tiffany's hand and heading back upstairs herself.

Butler, Rose and DA Joseph Harrison sat in Joe's office trying to figure out the best way to proceed with their main suspect, Marquis "Mayo" Harper.

"Do we have enough for a warrant yet?" Det. Butler asked detective Rose, who was finishing up the paperwork to present to the judge.

"We got enough to get a warrant for questioning," she said, passing him the affidavit for the warrant.

"I think we have enough information to bring him in for questioning, but I think that's all we got," Butler explained.

He wanted to make sure the case was a slam dunk before he made the arrest, but the DA. already felt like he had enough to get a conviction.

"Look, Detectives, I been doin this for a very long time" the DA began. "I got a neighbor who saw him leave the house with Ms. Thompson that evening. I got a truck driver who can, at the very least, identify the kind of car he watched a man toss her dead body out of. That car happens to be the same kind of car that's registered to Mr. Harper," DA Harrison broke down. "If that's not enough for me to get a guilty verdict, then I shouldn't be a DA."

After hearing it come out of his mouth, the case sounded a little more solid than before. Both Butler and Rose agreed. "So what do you wanna do?" Butler asked.

"Bring him in," Harrison said, then walked out of his office.

"I understand what the DA is saying, however, I'm not gonna lie, Emma. I think we're gonna need more," Butler said, calling Det. Rose by her first name. "Once we get him in here, I'm not tryin' to let him go. And looking at his criminal history, I'm sure he's gonna lawyer up before giving a statement."

Butler was one hundred percent right about Mayo. He'd been through the wringer when it came down to the justice system. Butler knew from experience that guys like Mayo were hard to prosecute. Before he made the mistake of messing up this case, Butler was going to be sure that all his ducks were in line.

Chapter 3

Niya pulled up to the apartment building where she had rented a two bedroom for Alexus to stay. This was also Niya's new stash spot, considering what took place with Chad finding the last one. Everything Niya took from Mayo was here, and this was actually the first time she'd had a chance to do inventory. Alexus was in the kitchen making something to eat when Niya walked in. Even though Alexus was still in her nightwear, Niya could see what drew Dro, and men like him to the young girl. Alexus had a small, long, shapely frame.

She couldn't have weighed more than 130 pounds, but she had an ass like a women twice her size. Her perky young breast sat high up on her chest, while her nipples protruded through the thin t-shirt she was wearing. Alexus had her long curly orange-brownish hair pinned up in a ponytail. She reminded Niya of Drea from Basketball Wives.

"I see you're getting used to doin' for yourself," Niya joked, entering the kitchen.

"Oh, I'm sorry Ni. I got hungry, and saw the chicken in the freezer and—" Alexus spoke, before being cut off by Niya.

"Girl, I was just joking with you. You better not be waiting around for me to come cook. Shit, you will starve to death," Niya chuckled. She looked over at Alexus, who had her head dropped to the floor. "Lex, you do know this is your home, also. You can eat what you want, baby girl," Niya added, now seeing that Alexus had taken her comment seriously.

"Thank you Ni, it's just that most of my life, I've lived with different people and family members, and I know how they can be about eating their food."

Niya could see the hurt in her eyes. She knew that although Alexus was young, she had been through a lot. She walked over to her and raised her head up until they made eye contact.

"Lex, babe, we are family now, and I love you just like a sister. If there is anything you want or need, don't you hesitate to ask me, and if it's some food in this house or any of our houses you are more than welcome to it. You hear me?"

Alexus shook her head up and down. Niya took her fingers and wiped the tears that were forming in Alexus' eyes. She then kissed her on her forehead.

Ever since the day Alexus had saved Niya's life, they had gotten closer. Niya took her under her wing, and also looked out for her on the strength of Prada. It was something about Alexus that drew Prada to her, and the more Niya hung around her, the more she could see why.

"Come on, I need ya help," Niya said pulling Alexus away from the stove.

They got to Niya's room, where Niya pulled the large sheet from under the bed, containing the contents from Mayo's house. Everything was separated first. The money was in one pile, the guns in another, and the drugs in another. Niya didn't know much about the drug game, but figured the brick-like packages were cocaine. The smell coming from the packages was so strong Niya was becoming nauseous.

"That's heroin," Alexus said, pulling her shirt up to her nose.

"Heroin. How do you know that?" Niya asked with a curious look on her face.

"That's the same stuff Dro used to bag up before he took it around to the trap houses," Alexus answered.

"What da hell am I supposed to do with heroin?" she said, counting the packages. "So what is this supposed to be?" Niya asked, holding up a different colored package that was wrapped the same way.

Alexus took the package and examined it. There was a little white residue coming from out of the side of it. She took some of it and placed it on her tongue. Her face looked like she had eaten a sour patch when she tasted it.

"This is cocaine," Alexus said. "Dro used to sniff this stuff twenty times a day. He got me to try it, but I didn't like how it made me feel," she said.

Altogether, it was three keys of heroin and two bricks of cocaine. The guns included a MP.5 sub machine gun, an AR-15 assault rifle, an AK 47, two .45's, two 9mm and a Glock .40. Mayo kept enough firepower in his house to take on a small army. Amazed by the size of the guns, Alexus stood in front of the mirror and posed with each gun, causing Niya to laugh a little; something she hadn't done in a while.

It took every bit of two hours for the girls to count up the money. It was broken down in every kind of bill. At the end, it was a little more than 1.2 million there, more money than either Niya or Alexus had seen at one time. They sat in the middle of the floor, just looking at the money for a while, before Alexus spoke.

"I think you should give Prada's grandmother some of this

money," Alexus said, breaking the silence. Alexus felt kind of out of place by making that kind of suggestion. "I'm sorry."

"No, don't be sorry," Niya said, cutting her off. "I think you're right. Part of all of this is Prada's anyway. I'ma give her a hundred thousand," she said as she began separating the money.

"Oh, I can't forget about you," Niya said, tossing Alexus a stack of money.

It was 50k. Alexus looked at her curiously. "What's this for?"

Niya just smiled. "That's so you can buy something to eat. O yeah, and for saving my life." Both girls laughed at the comment.

Gwen sat in the apartment staring at a picture of JR all day. His funeral wasn't until tomorrow, but Gwen felt like it was happening right now, the way she was crying. The last time she'd been in love with a man was when her and Chad was together. A light knock at the door snapped her out of her daze. Even though she was mourning, she was still on high alert. People trying to kidnap her, folks breaking into her apartment, and a boyfriend who was just shot to death, all kept her on her toes. She had just dropped Zion off to Chad, so it was no reason for anybody to be knocking at her door, lightly at that. Gwen reached between the cushions of her couch and pulled the chrome .45 out, then tippy-toed to the door.

"Who is it?" she yelled, pointing the barrel through the peephole.

"Aye, it's Mayo, Gwen. I need to talk to you," he announced in a non-threatening manner.

"Give me a second, Mayo," Gwen said, running to her room to put some pants on.

When she opened the door, she could see the stress written all over his face. Gwen figured it was because of the funeral tomorrow, but it wasn't. It was something a little more serious. He didn't even know where to begin, or even if it was safe to talk to Gwen, but at this point he felt like he really didn't have anywhere else to go. At least nowhere else he would feel safe. Mayo could see the comfort that Gwen brought, just like JR had told him about. JR would always brag that he had the best of both worlds, because even though Gwen's body was country thick with measurements of 36-24-42, she had the ability to show the demeanor of a caring young woman one minute, then fight and go hard like a gangsta who was 7 feet, 300 pounds the next.

"What's goin on, Mayo?" Gwen asked, taking a seat on the arm of the couch.

"Everything's bad. I pretty much lost everything. I don't have a muthafuckin dime to my name. On top of that, my lawyer told me that I got a warrant out for my arrest, for murder." he explained. "They probably think I had something to do with JR's death."

This was the perfect opportunity for Gwen to get some understanding about what had exactly happened with her boyfriend. The first time he and the crew came by to tell her about JR's death, Mayo really didn't want to talk about it, and barely answered their questions. But now, Gwen could see that he was vulnerable, so she began quizzing him.

"Mayo, I know you're goin through some shit right now, but can you tell me what happened to my man?" Gwen asked in a low, sad and sincere way. "I think I got the right to know," she said, now taking a seat on the couch right next to him.

He became quiet for a moment. He had recapped the whole night a thousand times in his head. "It was some chicks," Mayo began. "First, they robbed one of my trap houses... I can't believe I fell for this bitch," he said, thinking about Prada.

"Do you know where these females are from?" Gwen cut in, looking for something to work with.

"Nah, but one of them had the letters MHB on her wrist. She's the one that killed JR in my house."

"Hold up... did you say, MHB?" Gwen asked.

"Yeah... why? Do you know someone like that?" Mayo said, turning to face Gwen.

"Nah, I'm just wondering what those letters meant," she lied. "And that's who killed JR?"

Mayo told Gwen about the last phone call JR made to him, and how he had the girl at gunpoint in his house. He couldn't understand how the female got an opportunity to kill JR. The more Mayo talked, the more Gwen just sat there and listened. He told her about Mike the realtor, and how he was involved with a girl that had MHB tattooed on her neck. It was through Mike, that Mayo knew Prada was with that crew. Mayo even told Gwen that he killed Prada, not knowing that Prada was like her sister. Everything else that came out of Mayo's mouth, Gwen wasn't tryin to hear. Thoughts of blowing his head off right then and there crossed her mind, but Gwen had other plans. She was going to use Mayo to the best of her ability, and when the time was right she would make him pay for Prada's death.

It took Chad over an hour to finally get the twins to take a nap. Even on his day off, he was still at work. It really wasn't a problem, though. He loved being a father. He loved having the opportunity to raise his kids. Every day he woke up and was afforded that joy, it reminded him that getting out of the game was well worth it. Falling asleep himself, Chad felt Niya climb into the bed and wrap her arms around him. Her naked body pressed against his back, and a slew of warm covered his shoulder. It had been a little while since they had been intimate, and it was more than obvious that they both needed it.

Chad rolled over to face her. Words needed not to be spoken, for him to know where this was about to go. Niya climbed on top of him, leaned in, and kissed him ever so gently. Chad couldn't resist if he wanted to. Her soft, warm body on top of him made his dick rock hard within seconds. She was so beautiful. It was as if his hands had a mind of their own as they fondled her bare 38DD breasts.

"I love you," Niya said, looking into his eyes as she kissed down past the center of his chest.

Once at his manhood, Niya took it into her mouth, making the nine-inch member disappear. Chad moaned from the warm, wet sensation of her throat, and the more she sucked on it, the wetter her mouth got. He could feel the spit from Niya's mouth drip down his balls and onto the bed. She looked up at him in order to see how good it felt to him. His eyes were shut, and his hands gripped the sheets.

When she finally came up for bit of air, it sounded like she was taking a popsicle out of her mouth. She didn't skip a beat when she climbed back on top of Chad. Her juice box was soaking so much she didn't have to guide him inside of her. It just slipped in on its own when she sat on it. Her pussy felt wetter than her mouth, and as she swayed her hips back and forth, Chad palmed her ass cheek with one hand, and reached up and grabbed her throat with the other. He pushed his dick deeper and deeper inside of her until she could barely take any more.

"I'm cumming Daddy... dis ya pussy," Niya yelled out as she sped up the pace.

Now, palming both of her ass cheeks and watching how her

titties bounced up and down, Chad could feel himself about to bust. Niya's walls tightened up, and her body began to shiver. "Aaahhhrrr!" she yelled, releasing her fluids onto his dick.

Chad also exploded, sending about an ounce of his thick cum inside her. He could feel both his and her cum running down his balls. It was exactly what he needed. It was exactly what they both needed. Niya flopped down onto the bed. Both of them fell asleep, hot and sticky, in each other's arms.

Chapter 4

JR's funeral was packed. He didn't have as many people there as Prada had at hers, but all and all, it was a full house. One thing his family didn't have to worry about was security. It was more thugs at his funeral, than a Biggie Smalls concert. Just about each and every one of them was strapped. These were all of his friends. These were the people who loved him. The hood loved him, and this was the first time Gwen witnessed how much.

"Yo, ma, sorry for ya loss," one man said to Gwen after he viewed JR's body.

It seemed like everybody that was there apologized to Gwen for her loss. She was shocked that people even knew who she was, especially since she didn't know almost anybody there. It was normal for it to be that way. In the hood, the homies might not ever really see her that much, but they definitely know who the wifey is. Gwen had to admit, she felt like a mob wife, and being honest with herself, she kinda liked it.

A knock at the door, briefly took Mrs. Thompson's attention away from the hundreds of pictures she had of Prada, layin out on the dining room table. She was surprised, but happy to see Niya, Diamond, Tiffany, Alexus, and Tiki standing on her porch. She felt comfortable around the girls, especially Diamond and Niya, whom she'd known the longest. After hugging and kissing everybody, Mrs.

Thompson led them to the dining room table where everybody sat. Alexus sat the large duffle bag of money at Mrs. Thompson's feet. Mrs. Thompson looked at the bag and then looked up at the girls.

"It's just a little something we all put together for you," Niya said. "And please don't be stubborn, Mrs. T., I know how you can get," Niya teased.

In Niya's heart, a hundred thousand dollars wasn't enough. She'd wished she could have given her life for Prada's right now. That's just the kind of bond MHB had with each other. It wasn't a person sitting at that table who wasn't hurt, not even Alexus.

"You must be Alexus," Mrs. Thompson said, looking over at her. "My granddaughter told me all about you," she said with a smile. "Ya family now, so if there is anything you need my door is always open to you."

Everybody turned to look at Alexus as if she was the golden child. Those words coming from Prada's grandmother meant a lot. Alexus wasn't even aware of what just happened, but in time, she would understand.

"Mama T., I want you to know that I'ma... We are gonna do everything in our power to make the person who did this pay," Niya said, looking down at the picture of her and Prada when they had graduated high school.

"Oh baby, I'm not worried about retribution. The good Lord is gonna deal with whoever done this," she said raising one hand to the sky. "He's goin' to jail baby..."

"Mama T," Niya said, getting Prada's grandmother's eye contact. "I swear by the God that you hold ya hand up to, that if I find him before the cops do, he's not gonna make it to jail," Niya admitted.

Mrs. Thompson sat there for a second. Her eyes began to water.

She smiled at the sincerity and conviction Niya had. She looked Niya in her eyes, and without blinking, said, "Well, you make sure his ass never get a chance to kill again," Mrs. Thompson said.

After the funeral, Gwen met up with Mayo so that he could help her get rid of the cocaine she still had. She wasn't too sure on dealing with any of her people, after the attempted hit by Master and his people. So she reached out to Mayo, to help. He was on the run, but still had all of his clientele, and a couple of goons on standby. Moving the product was the least of Mayo's worries. He really just wanted to get his money up, and then get out of town before he went to jail. Gwen was all for taking advantage of his situation.

She saw it as an opportunity, especially when Mayo offered Gwen his connect after he got his bread up, and right before he skipped town. That was potentially big for her, it would mean no more middle man jacking the prices up. No more being one of the people caught up in the drought. No more having to worry about owing anybody. Gwen was gonna be free, and well enough in a position to take over the city. She loved the idea of not only being her own boss, but everybody else's boss as well.

"Now, this little spot belongs to a nigga named Dollaz," Mayo said, pulling up to the corner of Cummings Avenue. "He's good for nine ounces a week, sometimes more," he told Gwen.

Just as he said that, Dollaz came from out of one of the trap houses to investigate the unknown car on his block. Gwen took his appearance in with one quick look. He was a lil Wayne look alike with dreads falling all the way down his back. He had on an orange T- shirt with the words Truck Fit written in black. He wore the shirt with some khaki pants, and orange and black LeBrons. Every part of his body that wasn't covered by the clothing was etched with tattoos. The one that stood out to Gwen was the "Thug Life" that sat on the left side of his neck.

Boldly, he walked right up to Gwen's car and looked in the window. He didn't care who it was, they was in his hood and on his block, so he knew if anyone should have had fear, it was the occupants of the car, not him.

"Gotdam, baby boy, what it look like?" Mayo said, rolling down the window and also easing the mood.

"Aww man, I see you ridin' in somethin' new," Dollaz shot back, looking around to see who all was in the car.

"Yeah, this my peeps' ride, I got her chauffeuring a nigga today," Mayo responded while pointing at Gwen. "You going to be seeing her more often, so I wanted to introduce ya'll myself, you dig?"

"Brah you know I don't care who bring it as long as it gets brought." Dollaz uttered back.

The small talk was over in a matter of seconds, and before Gwen knew it, she was serving Dollaz nine ounces of powder cocaine. This was the first of many more transactions to come. The only thing Gwen didn't like, was when Mayo introduced her as his girl. She was about to correct him, but realized that was something so small compared to the big picture.

After leaving Prada's Mom's house, Tiffany, Diamond, Alexus, and Niya went back to Alexus' apartment. The girls sat at the kitchen table in silence, waiting for Niya to come out of her room. Niya had to think long and hard about what she was about to get herself into. She had to weigh the option on herself before she could ask anybody else to join her.

It took half an hour for her to emerge from her room with a book bag over her shoulder. She tossed the bag on the table, and took a seat at the head. Still, everyone was unaware of where she was going.

"I want ya'll to understand that this is a very difficult task that I'm about to ask you to do," Niya began. "I love each and every one of ya'll like you were my own flesh-n-blood..."

"Ni, what's goin on?" Diamond interrupted, feeling like something was wrong.

"Let me finish... let me finish," Niya said, holding a finger up. "Look, I'm tired of struggling, I'm tired of wasting my time runnin' around this city tryin' to set niggas up. I'm tired of wishing and dreaming to own my own club, and every day I wake up, I get pushed farther and farther away from my goal."

Diamond could tell that Niya was serious. She never heard her speak with so much passion before. Tiffany felt the same way. This was the first time she saw Niya in this form. Niya stood up from her chair and grabbed the bag. She emptied the contents of it onto the table. It was the three keys of heroin and the two bricks of cocaine. Diamond looked at the packages, and then back at Niya. Tiffany grabbed one of the bricks of cocaine and started to examine it.

"I'm tryin' to get into the game," Niya announced, looking around the room.

"The drug game?" Tiffany asked, staring at the brick.

"Yeah, the drug game." Niya shot back. "I'm not just tryin' to get in the drug game, I'm tryin' to take over," she declared.

Niya came to the conclusion that it was going to be all or nothing. It was no point being in the streets if you wasn't gonna go hard.

"What about dese niggas out here? You know they not gonna just let us sell drugs in their hood," Diamond said, picking up one of the bricks.

Niya nodded to Alexus. She got right up from the table, went into Niya's room, and came back out with the Ak-47 in her hands, and two of the handguns sticking out of her pockets.

Diamond looked over at Niya. "You serious Ni?" she asked.

"As I ever been," Niya replied with a stern look on her face. "So what ya'll wanna do?"

The whole apartment became silent. Diamond and Tiffany looked off into space for a moment. It didn't take Diamond long to come up with her answer. It was a proven fact that it was nothing she wouldn't do for MHB. Not only that, but she liked the idea of competing with the same niggas in the hood she used to run around chasing.

"Fuck it, I'm wit you," Diamond said, pulling one of the handguns from Alexus' pocket.

"Ya'll bitches ain't gonna leave me out of the picture!" Tiffany said, grabbing the other handgun from Alexus' pocket.

Niya looked around the room, and was satisfied with who she had on her team. This was the start of a new beginning for MHB, and if Charlotte was sleeping on the abilities of the women, MHB was about to wake the town up.

"Search Warrant!" Detective Butler yelled before kicking Mayo's front door off the hinges.

He led the tactical unit inside of the house, clearing each room of the house. Detective Butler had a feeling Mayo wasn't going to be there, but decided to be sure of it. Once Mayo got the heads-up from his lawyer that a warrant was being issued for his arrest, he never even thought about goin back home.

"He's still in the city. I can feel it," Butler told Det. Rose as they stood in the center of Mayo's front lawn.

"Yeah, well we got plenty of doors to kick in today, and I'm sure he's gonna be in one of them," Rose said, walking back to the car.

It was an all-day affair, kicking in door after door, looking for Mayo. They went any and everywhere he'd lived before he had become a target for the detectives. They even got the green light from the District Attorney to raid several of his known trap houses, information courtesy of an informant. It was pretty much an all-out manhunt, and if Mayo was still in the city, it wouldn't be much longer until he ran into the people who was looking for him.

It was some unfinished business Gwen had to deal with before she could hit the streets, full-fledge, and Niya was at the top of her list. She knew for sure now, that Niya had killed JR, and a need for revenge was running through her brain. At the same time, she struggled with her heart. She wasn't sure if she could actually commit the act of killing Niya. So much had happened over the years, and the wedge between them had gotten uglier. But the fact still remained that she held some love for Niya, and more importantly, they both made the oath never to put anything before MHB, not even a nigga. Gwen honestly didn't know what she was going to do, but one thing was for sure, and that was Niya had to answer in some kind of way for killing JR.

The traffic light turned from green to yellow, but Mayo wasn't stupid enough to go through it, considering his delicate situation. He'd never been this cautious in his life, and before long, his caution turned into paranoia. Every cop car he saw, his heart just about jumped out of his chest. The only reason he was doing his own driving now, was because Gwen had to pick her son up. Mayo had some important errands to run. It was still a lot of money on the streets that belonged to him, and he needed every bit of it.

While sitting at the light, Mayo glanced in the rear view mirror and noticed a cop car pulling up a few cars back. His paranoia kicked into overdrive. The cop car wasn't even thinking about him, nor did his rental car draw any attention. If the cops had been looking for him to be in any car, it would have been the Benz.

"Shit," he mumbled to himself, turning on his turn signal to make a right turn when the light changed. He was trying so hard to avoid the cop car, he didn't even notice that the cop had his turn signal on to make the right at the light. All Mayo had to do was keep going straight ahead, but as soon as the light turned green, he made a right.

Moments later, the cop car made the same right turn. Mayo almost defecated on himself when he saw the cop car behind him. He looked to turn into a little shopping center, and actually made the gesture of turning, but turned his wheel back and decided to keep going straight. That motion along with the fact that he was black, made the officer turn his lights on for Mayo to pull over. When Mayo pulled to the side of the road, he reached under his seat and grabbed the 9mm. He looked in the rearview again to see if the cop was alone, or if he had a partner.

Mayo wasn't tryin to go to jail, but if he didn't do something now, he wasn't going to have much of a choice. His chances of getting away were getting slimmer by the second. They grew even slimmer when two police officers got out of the car. Everything was happening so fast. It would be suicide if he got out of the car and started shooting now, and he knew it. He waited for the officers to get as close as his back doors, then threw the car in drive and stepped on the gas. The officers got back in their cars and began the pursuit. Mayo punched it, but his efforts were put to a halt when a car shot out of the mall's parking lot, Mayo slammed on the brakes but it was too late.

He crashed into the back end of the car and spun out of control. His car hit the pavement and turned over. His body was slung around like a ragdoll. The only thing he could hear before he passed out was the sound of the two cops yelling, "Do not move!"

Det. Butler got the call that Marquis Harper was in custody and had been taken to nearby hospital after the car crash. Butler and Rose were at the hospital within minutes of the call. They had expected for his apprehension to be a little different than this, which would have included multiple shots being fired, and somebody, if not him, being killed.

"How long has he been out?" Det. Butler asked the officer outside of his door when he walked up.

"Ever since the accident. The doctor said that he should be fine, though." the officer answered.

Butler relieved the officer, grabbed a chair, and sat it right next to Mayo's bed. He was going to make sure that vhe was the first person Mayo saw when he woke up, and it would be then that the real party would start.

Chapter 5

Niya didn't know the first thing about heroin, or where to begin, for that matter. The heroin game was a whole lot different from the cocaine game. There were a lot of problems that came along with it, mainly the amount of time one could get for selling it. The risk was greater, but the money was crazy. A key of heroin cost about 80k, while a brick of cocaine went for 20k.

"So you sure you know what your doin?" Niya asked Mandy, watching her crack open one of the keys of heroin. Mandy was an old friend from back in the day when Niya used to live in the projects. Mandy had moved to Betty Ford Rd. after high school, and had been there ever since. She knew so much about heroin because that's all her neighborhood was known for. Betty Ford Rd. was the most violent street in Charlotte, because of the heroin trade. Heroin junkies were worse than crackheads. A crackhead could go cold turkey and quit, but A Heroin addict would need years of treatment and methadone shots to kick the habit.

"Look, I'ma put you on to my cousin. He got this neighborhood on lock down," Mandy spoke through the mask as she blended in the cut to the heroin. "If you sell it right, you can come up around here girl," she joked.

"Who's ya cousin?" Niya asked, not really up for dealing with people she didn't know.

"His name is Master. He just got out of the hospital. I'ma walk you over there when I get done."

It had taken her a while, but Mandy had cut up a whole key of heroin for Niya. She even broke it down into ounces so that it would be easier for Niya to manage if she chose to just sell weight. The prices were the only thing left to discuss, which again, Niya had no knowledge of. However, with her messing around with Mandy, she was definitely about to get a crash course on the dope game.

Gwen checked to make sure she had a bullet in the chamber before getting out of the car. Master must've been crazy to think that the beef was over between him and her. She had made her mind up a long time ago, that Master had to go for pulling that stunt. Gwen just wouldn't be able to sleep right, knowing that he was out there healing from his wounds, and would be up and rolling again in a short time. Her phone started ringing the moment she got out of the car, and her first thought was not to answer it, but then she remembered that she was waiting on a specific call.

"Yeah," Gwen answered, tucking the .45 into her back pocket.

It was exactly who she thought it might have been. She quickly accepted the call from the county jail, knowing that it could only be one person.

"Yo shawty, what's good wit you?" Mayo said.

"Nothin' much. I'm just about to go and take care of something," Gwen said, looking down the street.

"Well look, I'm not gonna do too much talkin' over the phone. My visiting day is on Saturday from 11-1pm—"

"Say no more. I'll be up there," she said, cutting him off. "Other than that, are you good in there?"

"Yeah, I'm good. I'll see what they're talking about when I go to court next week. But look, I was just checkin' up on you. We'll talk when I see you," Mayo said before hanging up the phone.

Gwen hung up the phone too, but this time, decided to leave the phone in the car as opposed to keeping it on her. She proceeded to Betty Ford Rd. with one thing on her mind. She didn't know what house Master lived in or even if he stayed on that street, but Gwen remembered that every time JR would bring him stuff, he'd be sitting on one of the porches. That's all Gwen was banking on.

"What up, cuz?" Mandy said, walking up to him with Niya in tow. "Yo, dis my girl, Niya," she introduced.

"What up, shawty?" he said, looking up at Niya.

Niya looked down at the short, dark muscular man. He had a baldhead and sweat ran down it, even though is wasn't that hot outside.

Master's words were limited, because he was still in pain. The weed smoke helped somewhat, but it was still hard for him to do things such as talk, walk, laugh, or sleep comfortably.

"Yo Cuz, my girl got some work she's tryin' to get rid of, and I told her that you could help her out.

"Oh yeah? What kind of work?" Master asked with a curious look on his face.

Niya stepped in and passed him one of the ounces she had brought outside with her. He looked at the plastic bag, then put it to his nose. The smell was so strong he caught a little contact. He didn't have to ask what it was. He knew that it was heroin.

"Where you get dis from, shawty?" Master asked, looking at Niya.

"Does it matter? I got it for sale," Niya snapped back. "Do you wanna buy it or what?"

Master looked at the bag, and then at Mandy. He never pegged Mandy to be a set-up artist, but Master was still cautious because he knew the police had been lurking in the hood lately. Betty Ford Rd. was always a target for the local vice cops. Master waved for one of his dope fiends to come over so that he could taste the product for him. Niya approved it, wanting to know herself, exactly what she was working with. The fiend took one sniff of it, then wiped some around his gums. After a few seconds, he was bent over with his head between his legs. His mouth was drooling with spit, and he didn't respond to none of the times Mandy smacked him on the back of his head.

"How much you want for it?" Master asked in a hurry. He knew that this kind of dope was hard to come by now a days.

"How much is it worth to you?" Niya said, looking to get some understanding as to what the prices were.

Master could tell from that simple question that Niya didn't know what she had, and how much to sell it for. He figured that she just stole it from her boyfriend, and was tryin got make a few dollars. Either way, he was goin to play the game with her.

"I'm sayin. Somethin' like this go for about fifteen hundred," Master lied.

The average ounce of heroin would run anywhere from two thousand, to twenty-three hundred an ounce. Master knew that, but Niya didn't. She thought fifteen hundred was more than enough per ounce, especially since Mandy just cut it up and brought back fifty ounces off the key. She did the math within seconds, and saw that she could make seventy-five grand off a brick if she sold it that way.

"You got a deal. Give Mandy that fifteen hundred, take my cell number and call me when you need some more," Niya said, flipping out her cell.

"How much of dis shit you got, shawty?" Master asked with his mind already on the angles.

"Enough, just hit me up when you're ready," she replied, then walked back to Mandy's house.

Gwen looked up and down the street a few times before she came from out of the cut. Seeing Niya talking to Master only made Gwen furious. She came from the corner pulling the .45 out of her back pocket. The gun was almost as big as her, but she was well aware of how to work it. Master was looking down at the dope when he saw a pair of AirMax coming up the steps. By the time he looked up, he was staring down the barrel of a gun, and on the other end of it was a woman he prayed that he would never run into again.

"Hey Master," Gwen said with a devilish smile on her face.

"Come on shawty, it wasn't like dat," Master pleaded. "You don't gotta do dis—"

"O yeah, I got to. You think I'm going to let a nigga who tried to kill me, live, to get a second chance at it?"

Gwen looked into his eyes before she squeezed the trigger. Boom! Boom! Gwen let the .45 cannon blow. All three shots pierced his forehead, knocking him backwards in his wheelchair. She then turned the gun on the dope fiend, and was about to pull the trigger when she saw that he was already dead off the dope. She turned around, tucked the gun into her pocket and walked off as if nothing happened.

"Oh shit girl, get down," Mandy shouted, grabbing Niya's arm and pulling her to the ground away from the window.

It was typical for shootings to occur around Betty Ford Rd, but this one shocked Mandy because they had just left from outside. Not hearing any follow up shots, Mandy deemed it safe to go outside and see what happened. Niya wasn't too crazy about the idea, but pulled the 9mm from her waist and followed Mandy out the door. Other residents were coming out as well, to see what was going on. Mandy took a couple more steps up the street and could see that a crowd was gathering around Master's trap spot.

"Master!" she screamed, running onto the porch.

Niya followed closely behind her. When they arrived at the spot they were just standing at less than thirty minutes before, both ladies looked up to see half of Master's head peeled back. Damn, Niya thought to herself, I'm back at square one.

Chapter 6

Diamond and Tiffany weren't taking any prisoners. In a matter of days, they already had a trap house set up over on Milton Road, and were pushing up on a few corners that weren't really established. Diamond took the lead role in moving the cocaine. She got with one of her old boyfriends, a young nigga name Dollaz, to help her cook up. In return, she gave him coke for cheap. There was a method to her madness. Her eyes were set on Washington Street, because she knew the potential it had after seeing the old crews make millions out there when she was young.

"How do you know so much about cocaine?" Tiffany asked Diamond, who was sitting at the table watching a couple of crackheads bag up the product.

"My Dad used to sell this shit, my Mom used to smoke it, and my uncles used to cook it in front of me when I was yea high," she motioned with her hand.

"Damn bitch, you were made for dis shit," Tiffany joked.

A loud bang at the door grabbed everyone's attention. All activities ceased, and the first person to get up to go check the door was Tiffany. Although Tiffany was cute, petite and reminded everyone of Rihanna, she had an instinct to kill without remorse. She was the quiet type that nobody would expect to do anything. Tiffany pulled the blinds back on the window slightly. It was a young cat, with Chief Keef braids. He was by himself, but she could tell he carried an attitude with him, by the way he was standing.

Tiffany walked back to the table and grabbed the 10mm, then proceeded to the door. Diamond motioned for the workers to finish doing what they were doing, knowing that whoever was at the door, Tiffany was going to take care of it. Tiffany took the several locks off the door and removed the large 2x4 from in front of it.

Ignorant to what was on the other side of the door, the guy pushed his way in. Tiffany just backed up and pointed the gun at his face.

"Whoa! Whoa!" Diamond yelled, getting up from the table.

The guy didn't even have a gun in his hand, and if it wasn't for Diamond, he would have been dead. He took a good look around the house at all the people who were there. He was acting as if he didn't care that Tiffany had him at gunpoint.

"Who ya'll bitches?" he asked with a confused look on his face. "Ya'll bitches trappin' in here?" he said jealously.

"Us bitches? Who da fuck is you?" Tiffany shot back, not liking his tone of voice.

GoGo was a local hustler who had just come home from jail and opened up shop in the same house a few weeks before. He had only a little bit of work that was given to him by one of his connects, who felt like it was only right to bless him with the drugs since GoGo hadn't snitched on him. GoGo had considered this spot to be his trap house, even though he hadn't been around for the last two weeks. He had been out trying to come up on a new connect since he had spent the money from the dope his connect gave him. While on the streets, he heard through the grapevine that it was some action goin on in the house. He came to find that it wasn't just action, Diamond had picked up the pace dramatically. Dealers in the surrounding trap houses were starting to feel the effect.

"GoGo, you don't run my house. I can have whoever I want in here," Ms. Daisy said from the table.

Diamond walked over and lowered Tiffany's arm that had the gun still pointed at GoGo. Diamond had known Go since he was a little boy, and she knew that he really wasn't a threat. She also knew that he was broke and trying to come up. But most importantly, Diamond knew that he was still young, and easily capable of being manipulated by the right person and with the right things.

Diamond walked all the way up to him, looked Go in his eyes with the most innocent face she could put on, and asked, "GoGo, you wanna make some real money or what?"

The visiting room was packed, and it took Mayo 45 minutes to get downstairs to the visiting area. The process irritated Gwen, but she knew that this visit had to take place to insure a better future for herself. Today's objective was to get his drug connect's information, so that she could start making her own moves. Since Mayo was booked for murder, Gwen wasn't even sure if he was going to do what he said he was going to do. But she felt like she had to take the chance. Besides, Mayo had to know that he was looking at a long stretch of time, and would surely need someone on the outside looking out for him. If he hadn't thought about it, Gwen was thinking she would definitely bring it to his attention.

"What up, shawty?" Mayo said, walking up and standing there like he was expecting a hug.

She really didn't want to, but she did it anyway. Mayo wasn't her man, nor did she care anything about him. For all she knew, Mayo was the one who was responsible fo JR's death. If it was up to her, his ass could rot in jail forever, but right now, she kind of needed him. It was hard as hell trying to find a supplier that did business straight up in Charlotte. Local drug dealers always wanted to boost the prices up for drugs they had stepped on a few times.

"I'm sorry, I can't stay that long. I got to pick my son up," Gwen said as her excuse not to have to sit there too long.

"Naw, that's cool, because I need you to get right on top of this anyway," he said.

Mayo broke down the whole situation as far as with his case, and what evidence the DA had against him. He expressed his concern about getting a paid lawyer, because all he had now was a public defender. Gwen sat there and listened to him, but really did not pay attention to what he was saying about his case. She didn't care. It wasn't until he started talking about his connect, that Gwen started to focus on what he was saying. She had to remember the name and phone number he had given her.

"Now look, I know that there is nothing I can do to bring my boy, JR, back, and I hope that you don't think that I don't hurt over his death, because I do. Me and that nigga grew up together, got money together, and did time together. On the real, that was my right hand man, and for that, I'ma make sure you and ya son is straight. I'm giving you my house, so that you don't have to worry about having a place to stay."

"Mayo, you don't have to do that..." Gwen responded with a surprised look on her face.

"I know, but I want to. You can do whatever you want with it, just to make sure I get a lawyer at the end of the day," Mayo said with sincerity and sorrow in his eyes.

Gwen wasn't prepared for this other side Mayo was displaying. For a moment, she could actually see the hurt in his eyes when he talked about JR. That's when Gwen knew that it was time to end the visit. She didn't want to generate any type of feelings for Mayo, not even on the strength of JR.

Before the end of that day, Diamond had GoGo in the trap house moving work. He was soft for a cute face. That, and the fact that he was about to be making good money was enough to get him on the team. This was all part of Diamond's takeover plan. She knew that no one could beat them on price, considering their dope had come free to them. Well not free, since it had cost Prada her life, and nearly Niya's too. But they didn't have money tied up in the drugs, so they were able to sell it at a cheaper price than everyone else, and able to pay a higher commissions to the workers. MHB was on the move, and Diamond was the main face on the streets.

For the next couple of weeks all she planned to do was push up on corners and run down on potential trap houses. Her motto was, either get down with the movement or get found not moving. On her way out of the trap house, Diamond's phone started ringing. She waited until she got out on the porch to answer it, because she didn't want anyone hearing her conversation. It was Mike calling, "Hey stranger," Diamond said, looking up and down the block.

Ever since Diamond had started moving the cocaine, she really didn't have time for Mike. It was during this short period of time, that they both found out that some feelings were starting to get involved.

"Hey beautiful. I was wondering if I could see you later tonight," Mike said, looking out of his office window.

Diamond had to think about it. Her mind was really on money right now, and tonight she was supposed to get with Dollaz about some business. She wanted to take this opportunity to try and get Washington Street, or at least set up a trap house a couple blocks over.

"You still there?" Mike said, breaking the silence on the phone.

"Yeah, yeah I'm still here. Naw that's fine. We can hook up later on," she said as she calculated a time that would be good for her. "How does 11:00 sound?"

"Like a booty call," Mike chuckled. "But I'll take what I can get," he joked.

They both laughed. This was one of the things she enjoyed most about him. He was so easy to get along with, and always understanding. But at the same time, she couldn't ignore the feeling she had in her gut that things between them weren't going to last. She had been down this road before, and she knew most perfect relationships were always too good to be true. However, this one was someone different. Mike was white, so maybe, just maybe this could work.

Gwen left the county jail and got right on the phone. She had already hit up the realty guy Mayo had told her to call about selling his house. Mike had told her she could easily borrow 80 to 90 thousand against it. She didn't know how far ninety grand was going to take her with the new connect, but she sure as hell set up the meeting to discuss it. She had a couple of days before the meeting, so until then, Mayo gave her the ok to collect the rest of the money he had left out on the streets, so that she could add to the pot. Gwen's mind was made up, and she came to the conclusion that she was going to tackle the drug game full time, with conviction. This would be her year to get paid and put herself in the position she had been hoping for all her life.

Mandy and Niya stood in Mandy's kitchen, at the table, breaking down another key of dope. It had taken almost 30 minutes to move all the half empty cereal boxes and the dirty dishes Mandy had all over the table. Niya was trying to hold her tongue. Any other time, she would have told Mandy that even though you live in the hood, the inside of your house don't have to look like it. One thing Niya could say for her mother, was even though they were in the projects, her mother always made sure their house was clean. However, Niya figured this wasn't the time to discuss good housekeeping skills with Mandy. She needed her to show her how to cut and package this work. This time, it was for street level sales instead of weight, so the money would be even greater than what she could have made with Master.

Master had been dead for a couple of days, but Niya wasn't going to let that death derail her from cornering the market with her product. Diamond and Tiffany were handling the coke, and she and Alexus were taking care of the heroin. Niya had taken one of the most dangerous and violent places to start. This hood was crawling with hustlers and thieves, who didn't mind killing for what they wanted. But Niya knew that this was also the best place for the quickest and most lucrative come up.

"Niya, it's a lot of shit you don't know about the H game," Mandy said passing her a mask to cover her face with. "It's a lot of shit that comes along with it, and if you wanna survive you got to be willing to act and think like a nigga," Mandy explained.

Mandy wasn't lying. She knew how the dope game was, and the drama it brought, not only with the dealers and the dope fiends, but also with the law. On the flip side of it, you could become a millionaire overnight.

"Now, you sure you wanna go through with it," Mandy asked before even starting the process of cutting again.

Niya shot her a 'bitch please' look. "Mandy... if I wasn't sure about this, I wouldn't be here. Now, if you having second thoughts about getting this money, then let me know," Niya answered.

Mandy looked at Niya, and could see that she was dead serious. She cut the key open, and spread it across the plastic covered table, while Niya grinded up the Banita, also known as cut. Masks and gloves were obligatory if you didn't want to get high off inhaling and touching the dope. Many people got strung out on heroin, just because of the contact during the cutting process. It was the fastest way to lose everything before you had a chance to gain anything. After about an hour and a half of chopping and bagging, Mandy handed Niya the shoe box of work.

"Now look, I got enough dime bags in here to last you a couple of days. After that, I'ma take you to the store where they sell boxes of them," Mandy said as she continued to blend the cut into the heroin that was still left on the table. "The dope you got right here is an excellent grade. I might be able to turn this one key into two keys, or at least one and a half keys, depending on how much cut it can take without losing its potency. Oh, and I got to put you up on the prices so you can make the max on ya profit."

Niya looked at Mandy, and was amazed at how much she knew about dope. She was like a mad scientist in the lab, carefully doing everything with precision. Niya knew for sure that she had to have Mandy on her team, no matter what her house looked like, or the cost she would charge for mixing the product.

Chad sat in the house, playing with Jahmil. He had been with the kids day and night for the past three days. Gwen had to attend JR's funeral, so Zion was also there. He didn't mind spending all this time with his kids, but even super Dad needed a break, and Niya wasn't a lick of help lately. She was rarely home, and by the time she did come in late at night, Chad was too tired to even argue. He had to be honest with himself. He was starting to feel like the bitch of the relationship. He was doing all the cooking and cleaning like he was a housewife. It was getting old real fast, and Niya was so far gone in her own little world, she didn't have the slightest idea what was about to hit her.

He had reached his breaking point, and asking Niya to step up and be the mother and wife he and the twins needed was getting old. Chad was really feeling like the best thing he could do for all involved was take a break and give the marriage some separation to see if they both wanted to still be there. He wasn't sure how he was going to break it to Niya, or even if she'd care. What he did know, was that something outside had a hold on her, greater than him.

Chapter 7

"Harper, you got a visit," the guard said, tapping on Mayo's cell door.

Mayo looked around with a confused look on his face. He wasn't expecting anyone, so he wasn't sure who would be coming to see him.

He took his time getting to the visiting room, but once he got there he almost turned around on his heels when he saw Detective Butler, and his partner, Rose, sitting in the legal booth. He looked around the room to see who else was around, and coming from the vending machine, was his lawyer.

"What's all this about?" Mayo asked his lawyer with a concerned look on his face. He didn't know what the detectives were there for, being as though he had already been charged with Prada's death.

"Look, these guys wanna talk to you. They might be willing to make you a deal if you can help them out." Mayo's lawyer said, passing him one of the sodas he'd gotten out of the machine.

Reluctantly, Mayo went into the room with the detectives. He only intended to see what they were talking about. He stood there with his back against the wall, while the detectives and his lawyer sat down.

"What ya'll want?" Mayo said with an obvious attitude.

"Mr. Harper, a man was murdered in your house, and we know that you weren't home at the time it was done," Butler began. "But, I am willing to bet just about anything, that you know who did it."

Mayo didn't know if he was talking about Dro or JR. "Well, just like you said, I wasn't home at the—"

"You're right, because you were out killing Ms. Thompson." Rose cut in. "Look Mr. Harper, if you wanna go to prison for the rest of your life, then that's ok with me, but if you ever want to see the light of day again, I suggest you put ya pride in ya back pocket and take advantage of this opportunity." She said, pointing at him with her pen.

Mayo didn't think about it as an opportunity. He knew that they wanted him to be a rat, something he never considered until now. Life in prison had been his only thought since the day he was arrested, and it was a sure thing that life is what he would get for Prada's death. This was his seventh offense, and third felony.

"Yeah, so what you wanna know?" he asked, walking over and taking a seat in the chair.

"We wanna know who killed ya friend JR in ya house that night," Rose said.

Mayo opened up the soda and sat there trying to convince himself that what he was doing was self-preservation, not snitching. This was by no means was easy for him to do. He had his pride and street credit on the line. But sometimes, even for a so called real nigga, there is a breaking point, and he had reached his.

"So, what's in it for me?" Mayo asked, putting all that pride to the side.

Detective Rose smiled, and motioned for his attorney to fill him in on the deal they had already discussed.

Gwen hadn't slept a wink all night, she was constantly tossing and turning, and the same dream, or rather nightmare was continuously playing back in her mind. It was nights like these that she wished for JR or any man to be there to hold her so she could fall asleep. Looking over at the clock, she read the bright red lights announcing 9:00am. She had been up all night, with no sleep, and to make matters worse, she had a busy day planned and she need to get it started soon. Realizing that it didn't look like she was going to be getting any sleep anytime soon, she figured she would grab a good hot shower.

Once she was in the bathroom, Gwen turned on the water to let it run until the water was at the right temperature. The room was filling up with steam quickly, and before the mirror fogged all the way up, Gwen took the beauty of her naked body in and smiled. She knew she had everything a man wanted when it came to a woman, and once she got the money and power to go along with it. She would indeed be that bitch!

Gwen felt so relaxed, standing under the hot shower stall. It was too bad she couldn't enjoy it a little longer. A knock at the front door brought her right out of her comfort zone, but she was well aware who it was. Chad was dropping Zion off for the weekend. She still couldn't believe that he had him all week. Chad was really trying to stick by his word of spending more time with his son, and Gwen really appreciated it. She threw a towel around her wet naked frame and rushed to the door.

"Hi Mom," Zion said in a low tone when she opened the door.

He leaned in, gave her a hug then went straight to his room. Gwen curiously watched him walk away, then looked back at Chad. "What you do to him," Gwen joked.

"We been up all night playing Xbox and watching movies," Chad said with a proud smile.

"O ain't that cute. I know he beat the wheels off your ass," Gwen jokingly said.

"Yeah he did." Chad laughed back.

"You wanna come in for minute?" she offered, stepping to the side.

Chad peeked inside and looked around suspiciously. He had never been inside of her apartment before.

"Ain't nobody in here," Gwen laughed, grabbing him by the arm and pulling him inside.

Chad sat down on the sofa and looked up at Gwen, "I wanted to tell you, on some real nigga shit. I am sorry to hear about ya boy," he said sincerely.

Gwen had damn near forgotten about JR until he said something. She had a depressed look on her face, but Chad knew this wasn't from JR's death. He had seen this look too many times during the course of their relationship.

"Was it one of those nights?" he asked, this time with an even greater look of concern on his face.

Gwen knew that Chad knew her too well for her to lie to him. "Yes, I haven't been able to sleep all night, and my bed was soaking wet from the all of the sweating."

Her eyes began to water up, and so did Chad's. He remembered all the nights of Gwen tossing, turning and waking up screaming with her body covered in sweat. It took nearly two years before Gwen finally confessed that she had been suffering from nightmares. Chad thought back to that night and the horrific story that Gwen recalled.

She was seven years old and had been sent to live with her Grandmother and Grandfather for the summer. She always loved going to Norfolk, Virginia even though the town was small. Her grandparents would take her shopping and to the nearby beach. The days were beautiful and sunny and she would always play with her cousins who lived there.

One night, tired from a full day of swimming, her grandparents took her to McDonald's before going back home. Gwen ate the happy meal and played with the toy on the short ride to the house. Her grandfather gave her strict instructions to go upstairs and take a bath. He gave her some scented liquid soap and the scented lotion to put on afterwards. Gwen loved the smell, it was the same scent her Aunt May wore, and it made her feel like a big girl.

Once she had finished her bath and put on the lotion, she got dressed in her night shirt and went to bed. She was so tired that she fell asleep immediately. She remembered dreaming about all of the stories she would tell to her friends and classmate's once the summer was over.

Gwen's beautiful dream was interrupted when she felt a body pressed up against her from behind. Gwen awoke groggily; unable to see anything in the pitch-black room. The body behind her tightened the grip around her small frame. Gwen was about to yell, thinking that the boogie man was real, but before she could utter a sound, a larger hand covered her mouth. She could feel something sharp up against her butt.

At the young age of seven, Gwen realized quickly that this wasn't a boogie man that hunted kid's dreams. She recognized the familiar smell of old spice cologne as her grandfather's scent, but she couldn't figure out what he was doing in her bed. Her grandfather released his grip around her body, only to pull her pink polka dot panties down until they were around her knees. Then suddenly, Gwen felt the worst pain she had ever experienced in her life in an area her mother had always told her to never let anyone touch her. She could not believe that this was happening to her. Her young mind could not understand why the same man who'd been so kind and caring to her was inflicting so much hurt.

Her heart raced as pain and fear encompassed her entire being. Her instinct to fight back kicked in, and she squirmed and wiggled to prevent the inevitable from happening. She figured that if she made it inconvenient enough, he'd lose his patience and it'd be over. When that didn't work, she cried and pled with him to stop, but he wouldn't. Instead, he persisted at trying to force his way into her seven-year-old womb. After nearly twenty minutes of fighting, her body and will to protect herself had been exhausted. It was clear that her grandfather wasn't going to give up until he got exactly what he wanted. He was finished in less than five minutes. Once he was done, he got up and told her to go wash herself up.

"You better not tell anyone, or you won't be able to come up here anymore, you hear me?" he asked.

Gwen didn't respond, she just went into the bathroom. Her Grandfather would repeat the same shameful action every summer until Gwen was 12. Whenever summer was close, her nightmares would start. Even though Gwen had often pleaded with her mother to not send her to her grandparents, her mother enjoyed the summers when Gwen was away. It made her feel like she was single again, with no responsibilities.

Finally, when Gwen was 12, her grandfather passed away, she would then over hear a conversation between her mother and her Aunt May. Her aunt shared that her father had molested her for years, and it was the reason she had ran away from home at such a young age.

Over the years, Gwen had taken the anger and hurt, and put it to use for what she felt was her benefit. She would use the face of her grandfather whenever she had to kill. It had served as a sure fire way for her to murder with no remorse. She promised herself that she would never be a victim again.

Chad had always kept the hurt and anger in his heart, also. He wished that cancer hadn't delivered the painful death he so want to give to Gwen's grandfather.

Chad took her in his arms. "If you want, I could hold you and let you get some sleep."

Gwen had to admit that Chad was looking good sitting in front of her with a well-fitted V-Neck t-shirt, a pair of Robin jeans, and some black, leather high top Jimmy Choo sneakers. The smell of his Polo Black cologne traveled through the air, lighting up the whole room.

"Let me go change real quick," Gwen said, remembering that she didn't have anything on underneath the bathrobe.

Gwen went into her bedroom and put on a pair of boy shorts and a white tank-top, no bra, no panties. On her way back into the living room, she walked by Zion's room. Gwen quietly opened the door just enough to see that Zion had fallen asleep on his bed with all of his clothes on. She shook her head and smiled, going into the room where Chad was waiting.

"What you do to my... our son?" she joked.

When Gwen arrived back into the room, Chad couldn't take his eyes off her. She looked so good. Her body was crazy. Even without a bra on, her breasts sat up like she had implants, and when she got into the light, he could see her nipples poking through the cotton tank-top. The boy shorts she had on were so snug, her vagina print stuck out like a baby camel toe. Chad had to adjust himself on the couch, because he was beginning to get hard despite the attempts his brain made to block out her beauty.

She came over and placed herself in his arms. "Gwen, you crazy," Chad smiled.

"What?" she asked looking down at what she had on.

"It ain't like you haven't seen me like this before, shit you done seen me naked. What's the problem? Do I make you nervous?" she joked.

She was joking, but Chad was dead serious. His mind started wandering off, thinking about all the stuff he used to do, and now wanted to do with Gwen. It seemed like everything was playing back in his mind, and the main thing was how good and wet she always was. On top of that, Gwen had mastered the Kegel exercise, so she stayed tight. Chad and Gwen had a chemistry like neither ever had experienced before or since. Chad could feel pre-cum oozing from his dick when he thought about Gwen's full, juicy lips wrapped around his him.

"Yo, I got to go," Chad said, jumping up from the couch.

Gwen jumped up too, but stood in front of him so he couldn't' leave. Somewhat ashamed for having sexual thoughts about him, she put her head down, but when she looked down, she could see the bulge in his pants. She knew he was hard, and that only made her even wetter. Her breathing intensified.

"Chad, I'ma keep it real wit you," Gwen said in a low, soft and sexy voice. "I'm horny as shit right now and my pussy been wet since I opened that door and you were standing there..."

"Come on Gwen—"

"No, let me finish," she said, getting closer to him. "It's not a day that goes by in my life, that I don't think about you. I miss Daddy's dick," she said reaching down and grabbing a handful of his member through his pants.

It had been a couple of years since they had sex, but every time Chad saw Gwen, he also had sexual thoughts about her. Tonight, it was more than just those thoughts. It was something different about Gwen that Chad was attracted to. Something that was better than just having sex. Chad looked into Gwen's eyes and could see that she was still in love with him.

Chad grabbed Gwen by her throat, pulling her closer. The strength of his large hands made her body heat up. She closed her eyes and waited for impact. His soft lips pressed against hers as he pulled her body into his. The kiss alone was electrifying, causing both of them to examine the inside of each other's mouth with their tongues.

"Zion," Chad, said thinking about his son.

"He is asleep," Gwen shot back as she began lifting his shirt up.

Chad reached down and scooped Gwen up, wrapping her legs around his waist. Passionately kissing her, Chad walked her over and slammed her back against the wall. With one arm holding her against the wall, he took his free hand and pulled off her shorts. His jeans hit the floor the same time her shorts did, and before she knew it, his manhood had invaded her nectar box. She wrapped her legs around his waist as he stuffed every bit of himself into her. Deeper and deeper, he pushed his rock hard penis into her. Gwen wanted to scream at the top of her lungs, but she couldn't. She didn't want to wake Zion up, so she just bit down on his shoulder and clawed her nails into his back.

"It's still yours," Gwen whispered into his ear.

This only made Chad go crazier, he kept digging deeper and harder until he felt Gwen's walls tighten up from her having an orgasm. Chad could feel the wetness of Gwen's nectar thicken. He grabbed one of her breasts while he prepared to cum as well. His strokes became longer and faster, until finally, he came, shooting his load into her waiting treasure box. After a few finishing strokes, Chad let her legs down, but Gwen was far from being done. She grabbed him by the hand and led him back to her room.

"You ready for part 2?" she jokingly asked.

Chad didn't respond, his face said it all, he wasn't going nowhere anytime soon.

"Ohhh, my God!" Alexus said as she held her hair high above her head and closed her eyes.

She jumped at the stinging sensation of the needle buzzing on the back of her neck. It was initiation day for her. Niya, Tiffany, Diamond, and Tiki were all at the apartment for the event. Alexus was officially becoming a member of MHB, a move that would change her life forever.

"I don't know why you chose the back of your neck for your first tattoo, girl, but you got balls," Tiki joked as she put the finishing touches on her work.

"She MHB now, she better be able to take it," Tiffany laughed.

It was a celebration. Everyone toasted to the new member of the crew. She had definitely earned her spot when she saved Niya's life inside of Mayo's house. But it was Prada's grandmother who sealed the deal, opening up her heart to Alexus. Today marked the start of a new life for Alexus. From this day forward, she was no longer considered a child. This was womanhood, and Alexus didn't see it happening any other way. She felt blessed to have been a part of a family that would die for her, a family that would kill for her, and if need be, a family that would do time in prison for her. This was the unbreakable bond. Niya was the first to start the chant.

“Am I my sister’s keeper?”

“Yes I am!” the others responded

“Am I my sister’s keeper!?” Niya asked again, even louder

“Yes I am!” the ladies responded loud enough to match Niya’s voice.

“Then what true sisterhood has put together, let no man take under!”

“You look tired. You should go home and get some rest,” Det. Rose leaned over and told Butler who was falling asleep at his computer.

“I done looked up just about every logo, and I still didn’t come across anybody with MHB tatted on them. I mean... I got MOB, MMG, and MBM, but when it comes to MHB, it’s like looking for a ghost,” Butler said, rubbing his eyes.

He was starting to think that the information Mayo gave him was false. Mayo couldn’t give him Niya’s name because he didn’t know it. He only knew Prada’s and the information Mike told him about MHB. In a city of a million people, finding MHB was like looking for a needle in a haystack. The only thing about Detective Butler, was that once he had his eyes set on something, he was gonna chase it until he got it.

Niya jumped out of the shower and tried to creep into the bed with Chad as if she just didn’t come in the house at 2:00 in the morning. She was under the false impression that she was going to give Chad a shot of pussy to make up for the bullshit she'd been doing lately. She slid under the covers completely naked and grabbed his shoulder to try to roll him over.

Chad pressed his body in the other direction. Niya kept pulling, until he gave in. Chad finally turned over and looked at her. He didn't have any sign of being sleep, in his eyes.

Niya leaned in to kiss him anyway, but Chad didn't move his lips. He just looked Niya in her eyes, regretting having to say what he had to tell her.

"This not working anymore, Ni. I think we both need a break," he said, wiping her lip gloss off his lips."

"What? Boy, you better stop playin," she said, leaning in for another kiss.

This time, Chad moved his whole face out of the way. Niya leaned back with a curious look on her face. She still wasn't sure if he was joking or not.

"Are you serious?" she asked, seeing that Chad wasn't smiling.

"Look Ni, we going in two different directions. I love you, I really do, but I'm not going to play second fiddle to another man, women, or the streets. I'm tired of coming in here having to cook and clean like I'm some bitch ass nigga that don't work. I'm tired of having to take care of the kids like they don't have a mother. Whatever it is that got a hold on you in them streets, has a tighter one than me, and I'm through fighting it for your time and attention. We had a good run... We got beautiful twins out of the deal—"

"Wait... wait, Chad," Niya pleaded, now realizing that this wasn't a game.

Chad was at the end of his rope with Niya. He felt that he'd already been here before with Gwen, when he decided to get out of the game. Niya was doing the same stuff Gwen was doing, by staying out late, coming home with money he knew he didn't give her, and having something Chad identified as guilt sex. That was the kind of sex Niya was sitting there trying to have right now.

"You can have the house."

"Please don't do this, babe." Niya pleaded.

"You can keep the car," Chad said yelling over her. "And I'll come see the twins—"

"Chad... Chad... Please," Niya cried. "I'm sorry."

"Niya, trust me, we both need this time and space. If not, we could lose each other forever." he said, then rolled back over. Chad didn't want to see the hurt on her face. He had thought about this long and hard, and as much as it was hurting him to do, he really felt like it was for the best, before he started to have a real hatred for Niya based on how she was treating him and the twins.

Niya wiped the tears from her eyes, and then climbed out of the bed. She was crushed, and she knew that their relationship was at a breaking point. When Chad said something, he meant it, and the cold look he had in his eyes said a thousand words by itself. Niya got up, and hesitantly put some clothes on. She went inside the twins' bedroom, and hugged and kissed Jahmil. She then gently pulled the covers back off Jasmine's sleeping body. Niya crawled in beside her and held her as tight as she could without waking her. She then cried herself to sleep.

Chapter 8

Curious as to why the crackhead traffic had slowed down, Tiffany stepped outside of the trap house to see what was going on. She looked up and down the street, and it was like a ghost town. That was odd, because yesterday Tiffany and Diamond couldn't bag up the crack fast enough. The trap house had made a 360 degree turnaround from doing 100 dollars a day, to now moving over forty-five hundred in a shift, and that was all in a little over a week.

Tiffany was a little relieved when she saw a crackhead on the next street over, walking towards the trap house. That quickly changed when the crackhead made a B-line at the corner. It was as if somebody was calling for him. Tiffany went back into the house and grabbed the .40 cal off the table and stuffed it in her waist before heading back out the door. When she got to the corner of the block, she was shocked to see about ten crackheads lined up against the wall and a young cat going down the line, serving each of them with little bag of crack. As they copped their crack and left, more heads walked up, doing the same thing. Tiff went straight into gangsta mode on him.

"Yo, my man. Ya gotta take dat shit somewhere else,"Tiffany said walking up on the young dealer.

"Shawty, you got me fucked up. I do my thing wherever the fuck I want," the guy said as he continued to make sales.

"Dis ain't the stuff from your house?" one of the crack heads asked, looking over at Tiffany.

"Naw, that ain't from our spot,"Tiffany replied. "If ya'll want that real shit we known for, then go up the street,"Tiffany yelled out to the crackheads who were waiting in line.

Just about all of them came off the wall and headed up the street, despite the younger dealer trying to push them back. The commotion on the corner caught the attention of a couple of guys who was standing on their porches.

"Shawty, what the fuck is your problem? Yo, you got me fucked up," the guy said, stepping closer to Tiffany like he was about to do something.

For Tiffany, the talking was over at that point. She pulled the .40 cal from her hip without hesitation, and squeezed off a round into his leg. The young dealer grabbed his thigh, but at the same time tried to reach out to grab Tiffany. She let off another round into his gut, backing him off her. When he dropped to the ground, Tiffany stood over top of him and was about to finish him off. She looked around and could see a couple of people standing on their porches. It didn't matter. That's just what she wanted. She had to make an example out of somebody in order to establish dominance in this area.

"Don't kill me... Don't kill me," the young kat screamed out, looking down the barrel of her gun.

Diamond turned the corner in the nick of time, running up and grabbing Tiffany right at the moment she squeezed the trigger. The bullet just missed his head, hitting the sidewalk instead.

"No... No...," Diamond said, pushing Tiffany back up the street.

The young dealer got up and jumped into his car, hoping Tiffany didn't follow. The dudes who were standing on the porch looked on, impressed with Tiffany's work. If they really wanted to, they could have killed her before she even pulled her gun out, but they really didn't like the young cat she had shot, anyway. Tiffany had gained the respect needed to operate in that neighborhood.

Gwen pulled into the parking lot of South Park Mall where she was supposed to meet up with the new connect Mayo had promised. She was accompanied by Rell and Browny, two of Mayo's boys who he'd put at Gwen's disposal for the time being. These were two men who stayed strapped, and wouldn't hesitate to kill anything moving. Mayo knew this was exactly what Gwen needed. She leaned against her car with Browny and Rell within a few feet of her, just in case they had to get her out of there in the event something went wrong. It wasn't that they didn't trust the connect, it was more of being on point.

"I hate when people are late," Gwen said, looking down at her watch.

As soon as she said that, two SUVs pulled into the parking lot, both were Yukons and both were all black with tinted windows. They stopped right in front of Gwen's BMW, making her and her two bodyguards look small. The driver of the second SUV got out of the truck, went to the back door, and opened it. He motioned for Gwen to get in the back seat without even saying a word. Browny and Rell stood between Gwen and the truck, like they weren't about to let her get in. Both men had their guns visible.

"I don't have all day," a voice yelled from the back seat.

Shockingly, the voice sounded like that of a woman, catching Gwen's attention. She squeezed from between her two guard dogs, motioning to them that it was cool. When Gwen got into the truck, she was greeted by a young, light complexioned, longhaired woman. She was very attractive, and was dressed in business attire. Gwen couldn't believe the boss was actually a chick, and for a second Gwen, felt inspired.

"You must be Gwen. I heard some good things about you," the woman said.

"Yeah, likewise," Gwen shot back. "By the way, my name is Brianna," the lady in the truck said, extending her hand for a shake.

Standing outside of the truck, Browny and Rell stood attentive, as well as Brianna's men who had gotten out of the first SUV. It was like a staring match between them, and everybody seemed to have their chests poking out to show dominance towards the other.

"Men," Brianna chuckled, looking out the window at them all. "That's what's wrong with the game now. It's got too much testosterone, and not enough finesse."

Gwen looked out at the window and smiled at the sight of all the mean faces everybody had on.

"So what can I do for you, Gwen?" Brianna said, getting back to business.

"Look, Ms. Brianna, I'ma be real wit you. I know about drugs, but I never been on this level of play before," Gwen began. "All this is new to me, and I pretty much inherited this," she said.

Brianna smiled, thinking about how she too had inherited this life. She looked Gwen in her eyes and with a look of concern and asked, "So, is this something you really wanna do?"

"Yeah, I want this... I just wanna make it worth my while," she said looking at Brianna. "I got 100k right now, so whatever you can do for me, I'ma make it happen as long as you look out for me."

Brianna admired Gwen's honesty. She saw a lot of herself in her.

Gwen came humble and respectful, and that was a plus with Brianna.

"I normally charge anywhere between 25 to 30k for a key of cocaine," she said. "I don't even know you, Gwen, but I like you. You got the same look in ya eyes that I had five years ago when I was on my come up," she chuckled.

The inside of the SUV got quiet for a moment as Brianna looked out of the window. Gwen didn't know what to think. "Gwen, I'ma give you five keys for that 100k. What you do after that, will determine whether or not you really wanna be in the game," Brianna said, breaking the silence.

Gwen didn't know how good she had it, by paying 20k per key. Cocaine prices were at an all-time high. Brianna could have easily charged 30k a key to anybody else on the streets. Mayo was even paying 30K a key. It had to be a female thing.

"Sounds good to me," Gwen responded, pulling the money out of the nap sack she held. Brianna motioned for her to stop.

"Look, Gwen, I like you, but this will be the only conversation you will have directly with me about this business, for a while. From now on, you will either meet with Kasey or my lady in charge, Selena. Once we get some time and trust under our skirts, we will sit down again and discuss new terms, if need be, understood?"

Gwen shook her head to let Brianna know she comprehended her words. Everything in her being was telling her that this was the moment she had been waiting on. The life she so desired was about to be reality, and Brianna was going to be the woman to put her on.

Ralphy looked around a couple of times before jumping into the back seat of the unmarked car. He was a drug dealer, turned informant, and had been for a couple of years now. The information he gave, normally led to an arrest and a conviction, which in turn, gave him a free pass to sell drugs freely in Charlotte.

"Give me some good news, Ralphy," Detective Butler said, looking at him through his rearview mirror.

"Yeah, I got something good for you, but I need a favor from you."

"Yeah, yeah, we'll deal with the favors later, Ralphy, just tell me what you got," Butler said.

"MHB stands for Money Hungry Bitches. It's a group of chicks that hustle in the neighborhood," Ralph informed.

"What do you mean hustle?" Rose cut in trying to get some clarity. "Well, I know one of the chicks just opened up shop, selling H on Betty Ford Rd. She might be small time, but business looks like its picking up," Ralphy said.

The detectives looked at each other. They couldn't believe that they had just heard that a female was moving heroin, and on Betty Ford Rd. at that. If it was any truth to it, they knew from experience she wasn't gonna last in that area very long.

"I need a name... give me a name," Butler demanded.

"Niyesha... Niyrobie... Niya... It's something like that," Ralphy said, unable to remember exactly what he had overheard somebody else call her. "I'll give you a call later with an exact on her name. But in the meantime, how about that favor that I need?" he asked with a smile.

"Yea what is it? Butler questioned with a pissed look on his face.

"Man, really it ain't even a real favor, shit I'm looking out for ya'll and being a good citizen with this one."

"Just spit it out!" Rose Chimed in.

"Ok, ok… well, it's this nigga name TJ who be hustling over on the eastside. I got his address right here and his tag number," Ralphy continued while passing Butler the paper. "He keeps dope and guns on him always, and I know the nigga's a felon." Both of the detectives' eyes widened.

"And what did this poor bastard do to you, to make you such a concerned citizen that you would point us in his direction?" Rose asked.

Ralphy just smiled again, this time even wider. "The muthafucker been fucking with my baby momma, and I told the nigga I had something for his ass. And the time he going to get when you niggas see him is just what that bitch ass nigga need.

The loud sound of laughter caught both Mandy and Niya's attention as they headed out the front door of Mandy's apartment. Niya looked down the street, and could see a crowd of her new workers huddled in a circle, cheering on whatever was going on in the middle. Niya, curious and wanting to get some control and order over her block, went to go break up the fun. To her, this was no playtime, this was money time, and she needed these people to understand that.

When she got over to the crowd, she couldn't believe what she was looking at, and had to do a double take just to make sure that it was real. On all fours in a doggystyle position, a dopefiend name Chelsey was allowing Max, a red nose pit-bull to hit her from the back. Max was humping away like he'd been there before. What was even crazier, was the look on Chelsey's face. It actually looked like she was enjoying it. As much as Niya tried to hold her composure, she couldn't.

Niya screamed out, "Get that fucking dog off her, are you niggas crazy?"

Her and Mandy started trying to break the situation up. Everybody was laughing, but Niya didn't see anything funny. She was still cussing and directing the men to break this shit up. Two of her workers began trying to pry Max off Chelsey's back, but he was putting up a strong fight. Niya and Mandy pulled Chelsey off the ground, while the guys were finally able to free her from Max's grip. Niya couldn't help but to wonder what would make a woman allow herself to do such a thing.

Then she noticed the dime bag of smack Chelsey tightly held in her right hand. Niya was almost ashamed, now realizing, that it was the dope she was selling that had this black woman, a mother and elder, doing what she was doing. While everyone else continued to laugh and joke after Chelsey got up and left, Niya was coming to understand that if a woman would stoop this low, then what would a man or woman do for the goods she now held. It was at this point she knew she needed to step up security on herself and her girls. The streets had already cost her one friend, and she was determined to not lose another.

In just three days, the block was moving over eight grand a day. "Yo... we're gonna have to find another stash house," Niya suggested as her and Mandy got into the car.

"Yeah, I agree. And we're gonna have to start having shifts for our workers, so we can put a hold to the excess people around doing nothin' but making us miss money," Mandy said, nodding to a dopefiend standing up against the wall waiting to cop his drugs.

It was understood that Niya needed to put the clamps on just a little tighter. Her presence was there, but it needed to be felt. At any given time, somebody on the block might think about tryin his hand at robbing Mandy and Niya. It wasn't just the workers on the block, it was also the dopefiends that Niya had to worry about. She just witnessed with her own eyes that they would do just about do anything for a hit. Killing her wasn't something that was too far off.

Gwen was paranoid as hell, driving back home with five keys in her truck and a .45 automatic under her seat. She made sure that she was careful when approaching traffic lights and using her turn signals properly. Rell and Browny drove behind her the whole time, just in case they had to become a decoy for the cops. Gwen picked up her phone and called Browny to let him know she had something else to take care of. He was cool with it, and just stayed behind her. Gwen really couldn't afford to make any stops right now, but this would be quick, plus it was en route to her spot.

She was about to be doing a lot of cooking and bagging, so she needed to go to Premiums, a store that sold just about everything that a drug dealer needs. As she drove down the street the store was on, Gwen happened to look over and see a familiar car parked right in front of the store. She knew that it was Niya's Range Rover from the Carolina Panthers sticker attached to the back window. Gwen drove by and glanced at the license plate to be sure, and it was.

"Dis bitch," Gwen mumbled to herself as she looked for a good spot to park.

It hadn't been a day, lately, that went by that Gwen didn't think about the attempted kidnapping on her, Niya murdering her boyfriend, and then catching Niya talking to Master. She was all but sure, Niya was the one who was behind the kidnapping. The only reason why Gwen hadn't run up to Niya's house and blew her head off, was on the strength of Chad and the twins being in the house. But Gwen vowed to herself, that if she ever caught Niya out on the streets, they would finish what they had started in the basement of the church. And this time, she was going to deal with her in accordance to the laws of the street if need be.

Gwen parked at the corner of the road, making sure nothing was blocking her in. Browny and Rell pulled up behind her. Neither had any idea what Gwen was up to. Gwen grabbed her .45 from under her seat, checked and made sure it was a bullet in the chamber, and then exited her vehicle. She didn't have any plans on shooting Niya, but she felt like she needed to be prepared, just in case Niya was ready to take it there. Rell could see the change in her behavior, plus the .45 she had tucked in her pants.

"Yo shawty, you good?" Browny asked also seeing the look Gwen had in her eyes.

"Just come on," she said, heading for the store.

She could see Niya and another female coming from out of the store together. Gwen started jogging to close the distance between them. Browny and Rell were right behind her. Pedestrians on the sidewalk started moving out of their way, noticing that it looked like something was about to go down.

Then it happened. Gwen and Niya caught made contact as Niya walked around to the driver side of her car. Mandy had also seen Gwen and her two goons approaching, and she quickly went for her gun. Niya tried to tell her to hold up. Although she knew Gwen wanted to start some shit, she also knew that she wasn't about to take it to gun play. Besides the fact that they had Chad and the children in common, they both were still MHB to their death. This was like a family who could fight each other every day, but would never think of killing one another, and would kill someone else, who did think of harming either.

Niya's cry was too late, because Mandy was already pulling the trigger. Gwen had caught a glimpse of the shine of the chrome 38 semi-automatic pistol Mandy had, and had pulled her own Glock .40, and was returning fire. Everything went into slow motion.

"Oh shit... Mandy get down," Niya yelled, slipping behind the car.

Boom! Boom! Boom! Pop! Boom! Boom! Boom!

Gwen was letting her pistol scream in Mandy's direction. Browny and Rell were also letting it fly.

Niya got low behind her truck, while Mandy took cover behind another parked car. Niya reached down, pulled her pistol, and began firing as well. All she could do was reach the gun over the truck and keep pulling the trigger. She and Mandy were sitting ducks, because they were caught off guard. The sounds of bullets knocking holes in the truck flooded the street, that along with people running and screaming trying to get out of the way. In a bold attempt, Niya reached up and grabbed the driver's side door handle trying to get it open. A bullet crashing through the window forced her to yank her hand back.

Seeing what Niya had tried to do, Mandy crawled to her feet and shot out from behind the parked car and made her way over to where Niya was. Mandy reached up and grabbed the back side door handle, opened it, reached in under the seat and grabbed a shot gun. She jumped up and started returning fire, covering Niya so that she could get her bearings together and possibly get the truck started so they could get the hell outta there.

By the time Niya got the truck started, Gwen was already retreating back to her car. She screamed for Rell and Browny to follow. Mad as hell, Niya placed the truck in drive. She yelled for Mandy to jump in. As soon as she was sure Mandy was securely in the truck, she took off out the parking lot.

"Who da fuck was that?" Mandy yelled, climbing out of the backseat into the passenger side of the Range.

Niya couldn't believe what had just happened. Never in a million years did she think that it would come to this, but now it was only one person that could save Gwen, and that was God. "That was a fuckin ghost," Niya said, speeding the truck down the narrow road," That was a muthafuckin ghost," she repeated.

Mandy looked down and saw a red spot on Niya's shirt. With her adrenaline still pumping, Niya didn't realize that she had been shot. It wasn't until Mandy said something that the burning sensation began. She reached down and lifted up her shirt to see a hole the size of a dime in her stomach.

Detective Rose and Detective Butler took a ride down on Betty Ford Rd. out of curiosity. They parked a couple of blocks away so they wouldn't draw any attention to themselves. Right off the bat, they noticed the heavy traffic of dope fiends going to and coming from an off street. It was almost impossible to see who they were getting their stuff from, without getting close.

"I think our boy, Ralphy, was right about this one," Butler said.

Betty Ford was a little more active then it usually was. Ever since Master was murdered, the violence had gone down, and it had become a spike in the financial department. The dispatcher screaming over the radio caught the detectives attention.

"Shots fired! Shots fired! All available units to Cedar street," the dispatcher announced.

Rose looked over at Butler with a smile on her face. She knew he couldn't resist responding to the call, even though he tried to play it cool.

"What?" he said, looking at her like he wasn't that interested in the call.

Rose put her head up and back counted from five. She didn't get to three when Butler started up the car and pulled off. His hunger for action wouldn't let him sit there any longer.

Chapter 9

Mayo sat in the dayroom staring up at the TV as Judge Mathis was giving some poor sucker a run down on being a man. It was hard for him to keep his mind occupied, because he hadn't heard anything back from his lawyer, since he had given the info on Niya and MHB. Also, Gwen hadn't been back to see him, he still didn't have a paid lawyer, Gwen's phone was turned off, Browny and Rell wasn't answering their phones, the detectives had been giving him the runaround, and on top of all of that, he was dead broke. He couldn't even buy a Ramen Noodle soup, and it seemed like his problems were only getting worse.

"Homeboy, let me holla at you for a second," a voice said from behind, followed by a tap on Mayo's shoulder.

Mayo turned around to see a skinny, 5'7, 150lb kid standing behind him. The young man was brown skinned, and had the image of a crown tatted under his right eye. He didn't pose a threat at all, and at first, Mayo sort of brushed him off, not really feeling like being bothered.

"Damn homeboy... you ain't hear me?" the young thug said, this time in a little more aggressive way.

Mayo jumped up, irritated and ready to set this youngin' straight. He stood in front of him with a look that said, 'Is this what you wanted?'. The young kid started walking down the hall towards Mayo's cell. Mayo followed, and so did all the other eyes in the unit.

Everybody on the pad knew that lil Terry was wild. He was small, but he put in big work.

"Fuck you want, homie?" Mayo snapped once he got into the cell.

As soon as he spoke, Terry started swinging. Mayo outweighed him by more than 70lbs, so he proceeded to toss Terry halfway across the cell, then slammed him to the ground with ease. However, what Terry lacked in weight, he made up for it when he pulled out an eight inch flat knife from his boot. At first Mayo didn't realize he was getting stabbed. It felt more like someone was pinching him, but then he saw the knife in Terry's hand with blood all over it. He began to feel his heart rate increase and his breath was shortening.

Mayo kept trying to throw punches, but his vision was becoming blurry. The fight continued or rather the stabbing continued because Terry just kept poking and poking Mayo every time Mayo threw a punch.

The loss of blood was starting to take its toll on Mayo. He knew that if he didn't get out of that cell, Terry was going to kill him. He took a couple more punctures from Terry, but he made it to the door, pushing his way out of it and onto the pad. There was blood everywhere. The guard on the unit saw Mayo's orange county jail jump suit covered with blood and quickly pressed the emergency response button. Within seconds, ten officers strapped with vests and beanbag guns rushed the unit.

The doctor entered the room with Niya's chart in his hand. The bullet went in and out, missing all of her organs but damaging a lot of tissue and nerves.

"You're gonna make a full recovery, Niya. Just try to get some rest," the doctor said before leaving back out of the room.

Niya layed in the hospital bed, and explained everything about Gwen and the shooting. Diamond, Tiffany, and Alexus couldn't believe it. They didn't understand why Gwen would go this far. Niya couldn't understand it either. In her eyes, the last beef they had was about Prada's death, but the fight in the bathroom was the end result of that. It wasn't cause for Niya taking a bullet in the gut.

"So now what?" Diamond asked.

"You already know what gotta happen,"Tiffany cut in.

"Naw... naw... whatever the beef is, it's between me and Gwen. I'm not getting the crew in the middle."

"Shit, if something was done to you, we in the middle." Alexus added.

Niya could appreciate her loyalty, but all the same, she knew Alexus wasn't aware of the love her and Gwen once had for each other, or the family connection they shared.

"Thanks for your concern, baby girl, but all the same, I'ma take care of that. Y'all just keep doin' what ya'll been doin'," Niya instructed.

Unfortunately, Niya didn't have the slightest idea, that Gwen was holding her accountable for JR's death and the attempted kidnapping.

"I know that now isn't really a good time, but I wanted to let you know where we are at with the work," Diamond said, pulling up a chair next to Niya's bed.

"Nah, it's cool,"Niya said, a bit curious about the progress anyway.

"Girl, this shit is movin' fast," Diamond said excitedly. "By Sunday, we will be done sold a whole key, and the traffic is only picking up."

"Yeah, soon we are gonna have to find a plug, Ni,"Tiffany cut in. "I know a couple niggas, but I really don't trust them like that." she continued.

Up until now, Niya hadn't thought about what she was going to do once all of the work was gone. At the pace Betty Ford was moving, she too was going to have to find a heroin connect. Niya didn't know one person who sold heroin in weight, besides, the people they had robbed, and it was no way she could go to any of them. The more Niya thought about it, it was only one person that came to mind who may be able to help her.

"Don't worry about it. I think I know somebody who can help us," Niya said. "I just got to get out of this damn hospital before I go crazy," she joked.

Butler and Rose raced through the hospital.

It was hospital policy that medical staff had to inform law enforcement when someone was being treated for a gunshot wound. Niya had come in late in the day, and it was busy around that time, so staff didn't get around to reporting it until the following day.

"Yeah, two people came in with gunshot wounds yesterday," the nurse told Butler.

"One was a Mr. Alexander, who has already been released."

"Damn it," Butler yelled in frustration, looking up and down the hall. He knew that generally, when it was a shooting victim, it was a major crime involved.

"Well can you give us his address or something?" Rose asked.

"He didn't have any medical insurance, and hospital policy is once he was stabilized he was discharged. However, the other shooting victim is still here, in fact she is located on this floor."

Butler and Rose made their way down the hall and around the corner where room 208 was. When they got to the room, Niya's bed was surrounded by Alexus, Diamond, and Tiffany. Mandy was sitting in the chair off to the side. Butler started to enter the room, but stopped mid stride when he noticed something that froze him. He saw the letters MHB clear as day on the back of Alexus' neck. The tattoo still looked fresh, so it stuck out.

"Can I help you with something?" Mandy said, looking at Butler and Rose standing in the doorway.

Rose hadn't seen the tattoo yet, so Butler had to back her up out of the room before they drew any more attention to themselves. The girls looked over, but didn't say anything.

"Sorry, we got the wrong room," Butler said backing out of the room.

"Tom, what's goin on? Hey Tom, what's goin on?" Rose asked as she trailed behind Detective Butler.

Butler didn't even answer her at first. His brain was racing a million miles per second, and everything had properly registered before he could say something. He walked back up to the nurses' station and asked for the doctor that saw Niya. Rose was still lost. She didn't know what was going on, but she could see the excitement in Butler's eyes.

"Tom," she said, grabbing a hold of him and making him face her. "What… the... hell is goin on?" she asked.

"I just saw MHB tattooed on one of those girls in there," Butler told Rose. "It was on the back of her neck, clear as day."

"Well, let's see what she knows," Rose said, turning around in an attempt to go back to the room.

"No, no, no, no, no," Butler said, grabbing and pulling Rose back. "This is our chance to get to the bottom of MHB. I don't wanna jump the gun on this one. Now that we got em, let's do our homework," Butler advised.

Rose caught on fast. This was about to turn into a full-fledged investigation, and given the circumstances of the latest string of crimes concerning MHB, this case had the potential of becoming something big. Rose and Butler both needed this kind of boost in their careers. For now, all the detectives had to do was sit back and see how it all unfolded.

Mayo laid on the hospital bed handcuffed to the rail. Three guards secured his room while doctors worked on him. The stabbing was vicious. Terry managed to collapse one of his lungs in the brutal assault. Altogether, Mayo had about eighteen holes in him, ten of which required stitches. Come to find out, Terry was part of the 704 Kings, a gang that was well aware of the Fifty Thousand Niya and MHB had placed on Mayo's head. They had intended to cash in and if Mayo wouldn't have made his way out of that cell, they would have certainly done so. Terry's whole intent was to kill Mayo and he was about two centimeters away from doing it.

Chapter 10

"Where da hell are you goin?" Chad joked, watching Gwen getting dressed in the mirror.

She looked sexy as hell, he admitted himself, seeing how crazy her body looked in the black and white Dolce and Gabbana strapless dress. The gold metallic Nappa sandals made her already fat ass, poke out even more. Chad had almost forgot that she wasn't his girl, and was about to make her go and change.

"Boy, I'm grown. I'm takin my ass to the club tonight," she said smacking her right butt cheek.

Chad looked at her and smiled. It had been a while since he had been out to a club, and he was damn near tempted to go too, but the reality of babysitting duties set in. He wasn't going nowhere with Zion asleep in the other room. That was part of the price that he had to pay for choosing Gwen's place to camp out, while him and Niya took their break from each other. Chad had been there for over two weeks, trying to get his mind right. He hadn't even called Niya the whole time. He knew the twins where fine, because Niya would have called him if something had happened. Gwen hadn't volunteered to tell Chad about her run in with Niya, and since she was unaware that Niya had been hit, neither knew about her gunshot wound.

"You been cooped up in this house all week, so tomorrow I'ma take my boys out," Gwen said, walking over to the bed and climbing on top of Chad.

Chad was loving the attention that he was getting from Gwen. Niya hadn't made him feel this important in a long time, and that's probably why he hadn't left yet. For a minute, it felt like old times, minus Chad being in the game. It was crazy how in a few days of constantly being around each other, Gwen and Chad just clicked back in to their old selves. It was less than a month ago that JR was alive and not even his recent death could affect a bond that had been built over the past ten years. Gwen had loved JR, and at times, she missed him dearly, but there wasn't a man alive, or dead that she loved more than Chad. Chad also had a significant amount of love still for Gwen in his heart. She was the first love of his life, and had given birth to his first child. For that, she would always have a reserved spot in his heart.

"Make sure you bring ya ass home at a reasonable hour," Chad said, smacking Gwen's ass as she straddled him.

"Yes Daddy," she chuckled, leaning in and giving him a nice, soft, slow, passionate kiss.

She could feel his dick getting hard through his sweat pants. She knew that if she sat there any longer, she wasn't going to go anywhere that night. Gwen leaned in and gave him one more kiss, then jumped up and ran out the door before Chad could grab her and change her mind.

Butler stood in front of the chalkboard with little sticky pads, writing down and pining evidence. The main topic and probably the only topic was MHB. Within a couple of days, he had managed to take photos of everyone that was in Niya's hospital room, including Niya herself. The doctor who was treating Niya at that time confirmed for Det. Butler that she had an MHB tattoo on her wrist. So far out of all the women, Butler had only found her with MHB on her wrist. That matched up with what Mayo had told them about JR's murderer as having a MHB tat on her wrist, and Niya was placed at the top of the pyramid.

Hospital records provided her first and last name, and almost everything else personal about her life. It was already understood that this whole case was going to be built around Niya, and anybody else that was under MHB was going to be feeling the heat.

Club Onyx was blazing, but it was as if everything stopped when Gwen walked through the door. This was her stomping ground, and all eyes were on her. Tagging along right behind her were Browny and Rell, doing what they do best, which was protection. A lot of people thought that she was there to party, and in a sense she was, but at the same time she was there on business. Every drug dealer from Durham to Fayetteville was there, and this was her time to try and lock people in. Brianna was a hell of a connect, and in two weeks of hustling nonstop, Gwen was ready to cop again, this time even more than what she'd purchased before. She pretty much had taken Mayo's clientele and branched out a little further, with the small clients she already had.

"Damn shawty, I been tryin to holla at you for a minute now," Boss Hog yelled over the music.

He had Durham on lockdown, but the prices he was paying were too high. He was paying 26k per key, and he was buying anywhere from five to ten key's every couple of weeks. If Gwen charged him 23k per key and he bought five in one week, that was a 15k come up a week for Gwen, because she was only paying 20k a key. If she could do that with five to ten dealers on a daily basis, Gwen wouldn't have to worry about selling nicks and dimes. She could just sell weight.

After a brief discussion, numbers were exchanged, and just like that, Gwen booked another customer. This was her real purpose for being there that night, that and a little bit of dancing wouldn't hurt.

She did that until her feet started hurting, then it was straight to the VIP booth, she went.

"Yo, you got a couple niggas who wanna holla at you over at the bar," Browny said, coming into the VIP booth with Gwen.

"Tell him I'll be over there in a few minutes," Gwen said, pouring herself a shot of Petron.

Gwen sat in the VIP area, taking in the atmosphere. Everything was going good in her life. She was getting money, she had Chad at the house, and she was on the verge of putting the whole North Carolina on her back. It was only one thing missing in her life that she wished she had, and that was friends. That was one thing she missed about MHB and the sisterhood behind it. She'd missed having people that were there for her. She'd missed that ride or die bond with bitches that was willing to kill for you or take a bullet for you. She really was in need of some true friends, who she could share her good fortunes with.

Niya limped up the steps to the second floor of Gwen's apartment building. She was still sore from the bullet wound, so she had to take her time moving around, or the wound could possibly open back up. She had barely been out the hospital a day, and had decided that she was going to pay Gwen a visit and finish what Gwen had started. Niya had tossed and turned on what to do with Gwen since she left the hospital. Although it was no doubt that they were no longer friends, she still had a tremendous love for Gwen. It just sat so far deep in her heart, Niya would try with all her being to forget about it. Even with everything that had went down with the Chad situation between the two ladies of MHB, Niya had to admit that she never thought it would come to this. She never in a million years believed it would come to one of them taken the other's life. They had fought together, cried together, and loved together.

Gwen was the only person who Niya was able to share the pain of growing up in a house where she was constantly being sexually abused by the boyfriend of her mother. Niya's mother had to have the relationship she was in a secret, because Niya's father Nate, along with his twin brother Norman, where known killers. It wasn't anyone crazy enough to mess with one of their ladies. Not only would it be certain death for the man, but also Niya's mother. So, Fitzgerald, aka Fitz would come through late at night and see her mother. He would always spend the night, and go to work from their house. Niya's mother would leave to catch the bus at 4:40 am. Once she was out the door, Fitz would make his way into Niya's room. The first time it happened, Niya wanted to tell someone, but Fitz had told her that her father would kill her mother for cheating on him. Niya was stuck. She didn't want her mother to die, and Fitz only took about 5 minutes. So she endured the abuse for nearly a year.

But then Fitz started to get violent, and one morning, he choked Niya until she almost passed out because she wouldn't skip school and spend the day with him. Gwen was the first person to see the marks on Niya's neck. She questioned her best friend until Niya broke down and shared the agony of her situation. Gwen seemed like she was the one who was being abused, she was crying, and Niya could feel the anger steaming off of her. Gwen devised a plan where she would spend the night with Niya, and when Fitz came in that morning they would together make sure that he never came in again. The plan worked to perfection because that was a morning that Fitz would never forget. The scars on his face and back wouldn't let him. When he climbed on top of Niya, she reached under the pillow and grabbed a small pocketknife Gwen had given her. She tried to stab Fitz in the neck, but he moved and the blade pierced his right cheek. The small sharp blade nearly tore his face apart. When he tried to retreat, Gwen was standing behind him, with a knife of her own. They both commencing to creating puncture wounds over his entire body. Fitz ran out the house butt ass naked, covered in blood. He never came back around, and when Niya had seen him again a couple of years later. He quickly turned and ran.

Niya chuckled at the memory, Gwen was her girl then, but all that was now behind them because Gwen had attempted to take her life. Niya was now at the point of kill or be killed, and she wasn't ready to leave this world. She pulled the Glock .40 from her Tory Burch bag, placed the bag by the stairway door, and proceeded towards the apartment. Niya had a key to Gwen's apartment ever since Gwen thought she lost them at Zion's birthday party a few months earlier.

Niya had found them, but didn't return them in case she had to use them one day. Today was gonna be that day. Niya cocked a bullet into the chamber, walking down the hall looking up at the apartment numbers. She got to Gwen's apartment and prayed that she hadn't changed the locks within the last eight months. It was like magic when she stuck the key in and unlocked the top lock, and then did the same to the bottom door handle bolt. She locked the door behind her once she was inside. The light from the kitchen provided just enough light for Niya to maneuver in. She didn't give a fuck who was in there, all she wanted was Gwen. She knew that Zion wouldn't be there since it was the weekend. Even though she hadn't heard from Chad in nearly three weeks. She knew that he always picked up Zion on the weekends, and she was sure he was still doing the same.

As she walked down the hall, the first door she came to had a spider man poster on it. She knew it had to be Zion's room, because that boy loved him some Peter Parker. She walked a little further and passed by the bathroom. There was only one door left in the place. Niya pointed the Glock in front of her, turned the knob quietly, then eased the door open. She couldn't believe her eyes, and it was as if her heart was being snatched out of her chest. She looked down into Gwen's bed, and there was Chad, sound asleep in nothing but a pair of Champion sweat pants.

Niya just stood there, almost dropping to her knees in front of the bed. She leaned against the wall for support. He left me for her, he left me for this bitch? This is where his heart is at? This is the family he wanted... Niya thought to herself, looking down at him. No wonder Gwen had decided to raise the stakes and take it to gun play. She wanted her out the way, and from the looks of it, Chad did too. Niya was crushed. Her tears wouldn't stop flowing, and for a second, her weeping almost woke Chad up. Her heartbreak quickly turned to anger, and then hatred. She wiped the tears from her eyes and then walked closer to the bed until she stood directly over top of him. She pointed the gun at his head and then closed her eyes. She didn't want to see it, but she felt like it had to be done.

Then visions of the twins popped into her mind, then visions of Chad playing with Zion. She had just witnessed Prada's funeral, and wasn't sure if she could make it through Chad's. But then came the visions of Chad making love to Gwen in the very bed he was sleeping in. The thoughts of him and her laughing at her lying in the hospital bed. Fuck it, she wanted to see it. She wanted to see the bullet crash though his skull. He deserved it. He deserved everything that he was about to get.

Niya opened her eyes to see Chad one more time, only to find him looking back up at her. She mustered up everything she had in her to pull the trigger, but she couldn't. It killed her not to, but she didn't. The tears started flowing down her face once again. Chad didn't say a word. He couldn't, and the guilt was evident on his face. Niya didn't speak a sound either, and started slowly backing away from him, until she backed all the way out of the door.

Chad didn't even attempt to get out of the bed. He had absolutely nothing he could think of to say that would set the situation right. He was also just relieved that Niya hadn't ended his life. For a moment, he truly believed he was a dead man. However, Chad did know that he was now dead in one place, and that was, in Niya's heart.

"So what exactly are you asking me for?" The Police Chief, Rodney Monroe, asked sitting at his desk.

"I'm pretty much asking you for everything," Butler said taking a seat. "I need resources, money, manpower, every kind of surveillance equipment we got. Most importantly, I need to be the point man over this case," Butler pleaded.

Butler was asking for everything but the kitchen sink to put into this case. After seeing everything that MHB was involved in, he knew that this was going to be something big. He wanted to be the one to bring Niya and her crew down before the feds got a whiff of what was going on. The feds were like vultures when it came to indictments. They would sit back, wait for local or state authorities to gather the hard evidence and then swoop down and take the whole case from them. Butler was trying his best to avoid that.

Chief Monroe gave in with a little more convincing, and at the end of the day, Butler got the green light to head the investigation. He was given everything that he requested and more. The Police Chief figured that one of two things were going to happen, and that was either Butler was going to bring them down the biggest cases since BMF, or he was going to lose his job and probably his pension trying. The Chief was fine with either/or.

Chapter 11

Gwen changed into the bathrobe provided by the day spa staff, then headed to the steam room where Selena was. She walked in, and was blown away by Selena's body. With only a bikini bottom on, Selena stood in the corner of the room dripping with sweat. Her stomach was flat as a board and her breasts were perky and rounded perfectly. Her long, black hair became a dark brownish color because it was wet and she allowed for it to hang down over her shoulders. This was Gwen's second time meeting up with Selena since Brianna had handed her off to her right hand chick.

"I'm not gay or anything, Selena, but damn you got a body on you girl," Gwen said, taking her robe off and hanging it on the hook.

"Likewise," Selena replied when Gwen took off her bra. Gwen's body was crazy too, so much so, Selena had to ask Gwen if her breasts were real.

"So did you really want to come to the spa today, or was this ya way to see if I had on a wire?" Gwen joked.

"Trust me, Gwen, if you were a cop, I would know. We got more friends in the Charlotte police department then you can imagine," Selena smiled. "I honestly felt like being pampered today. In this business, it's hard to find some time, you know. Like now, even though I am trying to relax I am, still doin' business," she chuckled.

Gwen sat there and listened to Selena talk. People lied when they said that most pretty girls were dumb, because everything Selena was saying made sense. It got to the point where Gwen started taking mental notes of their conversation. In a way, Gwen was being schooled. That was big, considering that Selena nor Brianna rarely took the time to talk to any of their clients. But Brianna had told Selena that it was something about Gwen she really liked, and Selena was feeling the same.

"So, how much are you spending this time?" Selena said, getting back to business.

"200k, Gwen shot back, proud of her accomplishments over the past few weeks.

"Damn girl you on your shit for real, right." Selena responded.

First it was 100k, then 125k, then 150k, and now Gwen was spending 200k. She was definitely heading in the right direction, Selena thought to herself. She didn't know that Gwen had this kind of hustle in her. It reminded Selena of how she used to be, and as long as she was moving the cocaine at this rate, Brianna was gonna keep feeding her.

Tiffany stood on the porch, watching the traffic going up and down the block. She wanted to make sure that it wasn't another hustler sitting in the wings, taking customers. The steady flow of traffic showed that the shooting in broad daylight served its purpose.

"Damn shawty, you run a tight ship around here," Toast said, walking up to the steps.

Instinctively, Tiffany reached for her back pocket, where Anna, her gun rested. She wasn't sure if Toast was coming as friend or foe, and wasn't about to take any chances.

"Slow down, baby girl... I ain't come here for dat," he joked, throwing his hands up.

His demeanor was calm, cool and collected, and his tone of voice was smooth. Tiffany could also see the gun on his waist bulging through his shirt.

"So what you here foe," Tiffany asked, resting her hand on the butt of her gun.

Toast couldn't help but to think about how sexy she looked standing there. She had on a pink lace bra under a fresh wife-beater, a pair of Seven jeans that showed off her curves, and a pair of Jordans. Her hair was pulled back into a ponytail, which brought out the few freckles she had on her light, brown skinned face. She was pretty, sassy, and a cold gunner, a combination Toast admired in a woman.

"Nah shawty. I just wanted to let you know that I'm feelin the whole take over thing you got goin on,"Toast said, looking at one of the crackheads pass by him, and go into the house.

"Yeah, well I don't see too many nigga's around here getting money. Why not jump at the opportunity?" Tiffany said.

Tiffany didn't have the slightest idea who she was talking to. Toast was a vet in the neighborhood. He was the reason it was safe to sell drugs on East Falls. He'd put more work in than anybody in the history of that block. The only reason he was letting Tiffany and Diamond do their thing was because it's what the hood needed. Not only were they bringing in more money through the block, they were also willing to bust their guns for the cause. Diamond and Tiffany were reppin East Falls better than the men that were under Toast. The benefits were great if the girls stuck around.

Today was play day for both Niya and Van's twins. The park was always the kids' favorite place to go, and believe it or not it was also chill time for the moms as well.

"What's wrong wit you Ni?" Van asked, seeing the blank look she had on her face.

Van and Niya were cousins on their father's side. Neither had grown up with the two brothers in their life. But their Grandmother, Mrs. Maggie had always made sure that her grandchildren knew each other. She knew her two twin boys where womanizers, just like their father, and had stayed in and out of jail most of their lives. So she always felt it was up to her to keep the family together. Niya and Van would always visit each other when they were young, and when the family reunion came around yearly, they were inseparable.

Once the issues of a new connect for the dope came up, Niya remembered the big trial her cousin Van's husband had went through a couple of years ago. It was all on the news for like three weeks, and Van had spent the night with her a couple of times when she came to visit. Niya figured that even if her husband, Q, was no longer in the game, he could surely point her in the right direction. So she had reached out to big cuz and put the meeting together.

Van asked again, "Ni, what's wrong with you, baby girl?

"I'm good," Niya said, picking her head up to see Van's son Khadir playing with Jahmil on the slide.

Niya had so much on her mind, that she didn't know what to do or where to even begin. She felt like Chad had betrayed her and crossed the lines of no return by being with Gwen. She couldn't help but to think about if she would have pulled the trigger and killed him, and at that moment, she felt like she wished she would have.

"I need a connect," Niya said, turning to look at Van.

"A connect on what?" Van asked.

"I need boy and girl," Niya said speaking the street names for cocaine and heroin.

"You need it or your husband needs it? I thought he was out of that life?"

"He is, and he ain't my husband, the work is for me and my crew. I need it bad, cuzzo, or I'm about to lose my blocks quick." Van was a hustler's wife so she knew how important it was to keep a steady flow of dope coming in. It was always competition just waiting for a chance to take over your clientele. Niya was family, so it wasn't an option of saying no. But she still had to ask

"Since when did you get into that?"

"Since I'm out here by myself with those two mouths to feed," she spoke pointing at her twins. She knew how to push her cousin's buttons. Niya knew that Van was as loyal has they came and it was nothing she wouldn't do for her kids or family. And shew and her twins were that by blood.

Van smiled. She knew Niya had added that to seal the deal.

"I see you still know how to work a bitch's heart," Van said laughing. Her and Niya high fived each other and both broke out with loud sounds of amusement. "Exactly how much work are you looking for?" Van asked, already having someone in mind who could supply it.

Niya explained how she needed at least 20 to 30 kilos of both cocaine and heroin. Betty Ford Road was starting to go off the charts with numbers with heroin. Word traveled far and fast if some good dope was on the block. Dope fiends were coming from everywhere. Niya was moving every bit of 25k a shift, working three shifts a day, and that number was still growing on a day to day basis. Diamond and Tiffany had the trap house on East Falls doing around 20k a day and that number was also growing.

"Well... when I get home, I'ma make a few phone calls for you. Just keep ya line open," Van told her. "Now on another note, what the hell is goin on, with you and hubby?" Van pried.

"Nothing I can't handle," Niya replied. "Nothing I can't overcome."

Van knew that was the response of someone who didn't want to talk about it, so she left that conversation alone and they started talking about the kids.

Mike looked across the table at Diamond who was eating the dinner that he had prepared. He had spent half the day preparing the steak and baking the baked potatoes and apple pie. He went to three different stores to find the right apples for the pie, and went to the farmer's market to get the veggies for the salad. He got so much enjoyment watching Diamond devour the meal. He wasn't that hungry, and this wasn't really the reason he had asked Diamond over. He had something on his chest that needed to come off. Something he wanted to tell her for a while now. The feelings he had developed for her sort of blocked out his judgment, but this was something he felt she needed to know, if their relationship was to go forward.

"I need to talk to you about something," Mike said, dropping his fork onto his plate.

Diamond looked up and could see the seriousness on his face. She thought for a second that he was about to ask her to marry him or something. The thought of him doing something like that made Diamond smile. Even though she would have to shoot him down, just hearing him ask would have been cute. Diamond stopped eating, crossed her hands, and rested her chin on them, giving Mike her undivided attention.

"I been tryin to figure out how to tell you this for a while now," Mike began. "It's a guy named Mayo who wants you and ya friends dead," he said, flat out. Diamond's chin almost hit the table when he said that.

This was the last thing she'd expected him to say. "What did you just say?" Diamond asked, only wanting to make sure she heard him correctly.

"I said this guy I know named Mayo wants ya'll dead," Mike repeated.

"Wait... wait... How da fuck do you know Mayo?" Diamond shot back with a confused look on her face.

Mike dropped his head and began explaining everything that had gone down from the start. He told her about the robbery plot, and how he knew that Mayo killed Prada. He told her about how Mayo knew about MHB. He even went so far as to telling Diamond that he was the one that told Mayo that she was MHB and that he saw Prada with them, that night at the club. Diamond just sat there at a loss for words. She really didn't know what to say. She had really started to like Mike, however now he was sitting there telling her that he was part of the reason why Prada was dead.

"So you mean to tell me..." Diamond started to say, but stopped. Tears began flowing down her cheeks.

"I'm sorry, Diamond," Mike pleaded. "I never—"

Diamond got up from the table and walked into the kitchen. Mike didn't even want to get up and go after her, knowing that he had really messed up. He just sat there with his head down. Diamond, on the other hand, was hot. She started thinking about Prada and how much she loved and missed her. Knowing that Mike had something to do with her death ripped through her heart. Then guilt started to set in, she was thinking that it was her fault. If she wouldn't have gotten so into Mike, he would have never been coming to pick her up, and would have never seen Prada. She looked up to the sky and pleaded with Prada for forgiveness. When her head dropped she knew that it was only one way to make it right with her girl. Diamond took a deep breath grab a larger knife out of the knife holder and walked back into the dining room.

Mike sat at the table with his head in his hands. He was so far gone into his thoughts he didn't even feel Diamond standing behind him. She grabbed a handful of his hair, pulled his head back. Kissed him on his forehead, looked him square in the eyes and sliced his neck from ear to ear. She had cut so deep into his throat that his Adams apple was dangling. Blood squirted out across the table, and pretty much all over the dining room.

Mike reached for his throat, but stumbled out of his chair and onto the floor. He died in less than a minute from all of the blood he had lost. She grabbed a cloth napkin, wrapped up the knife and placed it in her purse. Diamond stepped over his body, grabbed the rest of her things and walked out the door. The tears where still flowing down her face. She had started developing real feelings for Mike, but those feelings could never be like the ones she had for Prada. Mike had to die and she had to be the one to do it.

Chapter 12

Gwen pulled up to Washington Street and beeped the horn twice, like she always did when she was serving Dollaz. On cue, he came out of his trap house and got into the car. The fact that Gwen was now serving major weight and getting real money, it was making her a little peeved with coming to get these crumbs from Dollaz small time ass. She kat this was most likely going to be the last time, so she had little arrogant demeanor when Dollaz got in the car.

"What you need, Dollaz?" Gwen asked as she looked out the window.

Dollaz noticed her new attitude, but didn't' pay it any mind. He just grinned to himself, digging in his pocket and pulling out a large stack of bills. Gwen still wasn't looking over at him. She was feeling herself a little too much.

"You can give me the usual, shawty," Dollaz said reaching into his other pocket.

This time it wasn't money that he pulled out, it was his gun. Gwen still didn't know what was going on, until Dollaz stuffed the 9mm into her gut. Gwen jumped, looking down to see the slide of an automatic weapon. She then looked up at Dollaz like he had lost his mind.

"Beep the horn," Dollaz commanded, nodding at the steering wheel.

"You must gotta death wish," Gwen said, looking in the rearview mirror at Browny and Rell sitting behind her in their truck.

"Nah... I don't gotta a death wish, but if I gotta ask you one more time to beep the horn, I'ma make sure you'll never be able to have any more kids," he said shoving the gun deeper into her side.

Gwen was mad as hell, but she did exactly what she was told to do. Once she tapped the horn, Tiffany came out of the trap house with an AK-15, running right up to the driver side of the truck that Browny and Rell was in. Browny and Rell were tempted to bail out of the passenger side, but had second thoughts about it when Alexus came out of the garage across the street with a chopper in her hands.

"Dollaz... you better kill me right now," Gwen said, looking at him with hatred in her eyes.

A tap at the driver side window caused Gwen to turn around. Diamond stood there motioning for her to roll the window down. Gwen rolled her eyes and did so, having much to say.

"Dis how ya'll ridin' D?" Gwen said, looking at Diamond with the same look she had for Dollaz.

"It ain't my call, baby girl. You'll get ya chance to holla at her," Diamond said, speaking of Niya. She then gave Dollaz a nod, signaling that he could exit the vehicle.

Gwen turned to look at Dollaz, but the last thing she saw was his fist. He almost took Gwen's head off with one punch, knocking her smack out cold. After stripping Browny and Rell of their guns, Diamond gave them ten seconds to get as far away as they could before Tiffany and Alexus opened fire on them. All you heard was the engine in their truck screaming down the street.

Niya Walker... Alyah Shaw aka Alexus... Daneill Smith aka Diamond... and Tiffany Grey aka Tifi ..." Detective Butler announced standing in front of a small classroom of plain clothed officers. "These are our subjects, and please don't let the innocent, pretty faces fool you" he warned. "You are not here to make any arrests right now. Our goals and objectives are to build an airtight case against each and every one of these women and anybody that is associated with them. You will all be broken up into teams and assigned to one of these women. If Ms. Walker decides to take a shit, you better be recording what kind of toilet paper that she used to wipe her ass. And if Daneill decides to have sex in the middle of the night, I wanna know the name she screamed out and what kind of sausages they had for breakfast the next morning," Butler yelled.

Once Butler was given the green light on this case, he turned into a drill sergeant. He wasn't about to screw this up for nothing or nobody. Dealing with people like Niya, Butler knew that he had to be at his best. He broke down everything from what kind of money they had to work with during the investigation, all the way down to the names and phone numbers of all five informants he had working for them. Butler was smart. He was starting this investigation right at the start of MHB's reign. This way he would be able to grow with them and watch their rise to the top, before bringing them down. One thing was for sure, and Butler knew this beyond a shadow of a doubt, and that was a guaranteed fact that he and the rest of the officers in that room were in for a hell of a ride.

Jamaica was a vacation destination, and was one of the most beautiful places in the world, unless you left the tourist part of the island and went into the slums. If one of the tourists traveled too far away from the hotels and found their way into the hood, it was a slim chance he would make it back out of there alive.

Niya and Van rode on scooters down a longer dirt road through the outskirts of Kingston. Niya noticed the way the locals stared at them and prayed that the scooters wouldn't run out of gas before they made it to their destination. The dirt road led them into a small village. Van pulled over and parked right in front of an old, beat down shack. Niya looked up at the shack and wondered how in the hell she was going to find a new connect here.

"Ingaaaa" Van yelled, getting off the scooter.

"Girl me gone kill ya callen me name like dat," Inga laughed coming out of the shack with open arms.

Niya just sat on the bike and didn't know what to do, until Inga walked over to her and grabbed her by the arm.

"You must be Niya," Inga said, walking her into the shack.

The inside of the shack looked nothing like the outside. It was nicer and more Americanized than anything, Inga even had tea ready to serve. Niya took a look around and noticed that Van didn't come into the shack with them.

"Don't worry about Van, she out back wit da dogs," Inga said, seeing the concern on Niya's face. "So, before we talk about anything, let's talk about business," Inga said, sipping her tea. "Why are you here?" she asked.

"Well Inga, I'm looking for a connect. Not just any kind of connect. I need somebody who can consistently supply me with Grade-A cocaine for the best possible price," Niya explained. "I also need for this connect to supply me with heroin. Not just any heroin, I'm talking uncut fresh out the opium plant type of work, and I need good prices on that as well," Niya said, sipping her tea.

"Damn mon, Van was not playin when she said you come direct," Inga chuckled. "Look, me gone take real good care of you. Van my sista and she say you family ..."

Inga got quiet for a minute. She sat back in her chair and put her finger on her chin. It was a lot to calculate considering she was more than likely gonna have to get the cocaine and the heroin over to the states.

"I can go as low as 18.5 a key for the cocaine... minimum of ten key per purchase a trip," Inga said sitting up in her chair.

"And what about the heroin?" Niya asked.

"Heroin come wit a lot of problems. I gonna have to charge you a little, more but I give you de best, so you make ya money back ... 100k a key is the best I can do right now," Inga said. "My people risk a lot bringing it to the states. You keep buying, we can talk about the price next time," Inga said in her Jamaican accent.

The numbers didn't sound that crazy at all to Niya. She had made close to 300k from one key of heroin and Diamond brought back 50k off one key of cocaine. In her eyes, the math was cool and the prices were gonna get cheaper the more they bought.

"Yaw good in here?" Van said, coming back to the shack with two pit-bull puppies in her hand.

Niya nodded her head with a satisfied smile on her face. "Yeah, we good. We are definitely good." Niya said, sipping on her tea.

Detective Butler got straight to business and had his team watching East Falls, Betty Ford Road, Niya's house, Diamond's spot, and Tiffany's apartment. The only place they didn't have surveillance on was Alexus' apartment. The surveillance team assigned to her never could seem to follow her around as much because she used public transportation when she wasn't with the other girls.

Butler and Rose staked out Betty Ford Rd., personally. Butler had become infatuated with Niya and the way that she moved. He put her at the head of MHB, and was determined to see to it that when it was all said and done, Niya was gonna fall the hardest.

As soon as Niya and Van got off of the airplane, Niya's phone began to ring. It was a reminder that it was back to business, even though the two-day trip to Jamaica was business in itself. The first shipment was gonna be delivered in three days and Niya couldn't wait.

"What's good?" Niya answered seeing that it was Diamond calling.

"Yeah, everything taken care of," Diamond said, then hung up the phone.

A big smile came over Niya's face. She had to quickly check it though, because Van started asking questions. Niya knew that Van had met all the girls of MHB before, and had a real liking for the realness of Gwen in particular. She also loved the sisterly bond the women had with each other. So Niya felt that Van would never understand why she was about to kill Gwen. For that reason, Van needed not to know anything that was going on.

Chad woke up from his sleep to the smell of smoke. It was so thick in the apartment, he could hardly see. He jumped straight up from the bed and ran straight into the kitchen to see a frying pan on the stove engulfed in flames. He grabbed the pan and threw it into the sink, then turned the stove off.

"Fuck is goin' on?" he mumbled to himself, looking around for the smoke detectors. The first thing that came to his mind was that

Zion had tried to make something to eat and went back to bed while the food was cooking. Mad as hell, Chad steamed down the hall, then busted into Zion's room, ready to whoop his ass. When he got there, Zion wasn't there.

"Zion," Chad yelled out in the house.

He called out his name a few more times, but still there wasn't any answer. He went into Zion's room and looked around. He almost didn't notice the piece of yellow paper sitting on his pillow as he was about to leave the room. He picked up the paper and began reading. The contents of the letter were so severe, it made him take a seat on Zion's bed. His knees became so weak he couldn't muster strength to stand up.

Chapter 13

Gwen barely opened her swollen eyes, looking around trying to figure out where she was at and how long she'd been there. She could taste the blood in her mouth as it seeped down her throat, and her hands became numb from the wire that bounded her hands behind her back. As she looked around the room, she could tell that she was in a cellar or some type of basement to a house.

The sounds of footsteps crept through the cracks of the floor above her, and before she could yell to her abductors, the cellar door opened. It was to no surprise when Niya made her way down the steps and walked over to the mattress Gwen was laying on. Niya had a large chrome .40 caliber in her hand, but at the same time she seemed relaxed. She was calm, and showed no signs of anger. In fact, she had a creepy little smirk on her face as if to say 'Bitch I got you!'

"Ch... Chad is gonna k ... kill you, Niya," Gwen managed to utter out of her bloody mouth. Niya just chuckled at Gwen's words, shaking her head as she walked up and squatted right next to Gwen's body.

"Do you really think for one second that he's gonna miss you? You foul, Gwen, disloyal and ungrateful." Niya said, waving the gun in Gwen's face. "Not to mention the fact that you tried to kill me. You better be lucky it's not him down here ready to blow ya fuckin head off."

"I didn't try to kill you, Niya. If I wanted you dead, I could have done it a long time ago," Gwen shot back in her final attempt to preserve her life.

Deep down inside, Gwen knew that this was her last ride. Too much had transpired over the past couple of weeks, and it was no other way this story was about to end. In an instant, Gwen could see her whole life pass her by, and the thought of Zion actually brought tears to her eyes. Even then, she still didn't let em fall, determined not to let Niya see her in the weakest state she'd ever been in.

"Fuck you Niya," Gwen screamed through her bloody mouth. "No matter how hard you try, he will never love you the way that he loves me," Gwen said, then spit a mouth full of blood in Niya's direction.

If it wasn't for Niya's quick reaction, it would have hit her in the face. The nerve of her, she thought to herself as she rose up, over Gwen.

"See, that's why it can only be one," Niya said, raising the gun to Gwen's head.

This was the end of the road for Gwen, and not even Jesus himself could walk down the steps, and stop Niya from pulling the trigger. Niya took the safety off, looked Gwen in her eyes and took a deep breath.

"Goodnight, baby girl," Niya said.

The sound of the basement door swinging open temporarily grabbed Niya's attention. She looked up to see the unexpected walking down the steps. It was like the whole world was caving in. But before she would let Chad change her mind about killing her, she quickly focused her attention back on Gwen. Now, anger showed all over her face. Her palms were sweaty, heart was racing, and her finger was on the trigger.

"Ni, don't shoot her," Chad yelled out. "Please babe, I'm begging you," Chad pleaded.

Niya stopped and turned to face him. He had never begged her to do anything, and the tone in his voice sounded like he was scared of something or someone. Niya took her attention off Gwen for a moment, to see what was goin on with Chad. He only had one chance to speak before Niya put a bullet in Gwen's head.

"He got my son," Chad said, damn near breaking down. "Da nigga Mayo took my son and she's the only one that can get him back."

"Noooo," Gwen yelled out, hearing Chad. "My son... Oh God, my Zion," Gwen cried, trying to wiggle out of the restraints she had on.

"You kill her, you kill my son. You kill my son, then you might as well kill me," Chad said with a dead serious look in his eyes.

Niya didn't believe him at first, but then beyond his anger, Niya could see the hurt in his eyes. This changed everything. There was no way in hell that she was going to be able to pull the trigger. It would be killing three people with one bullet, a heavy price to pay for such a selfish act. She lowered her gun, tucked it into her back pocket and headed for the steps. She stopped at Chad.

"For what it's worth, I hope you find ya son... ya family needs you," Niya said, looking back at Gwen, then turned around and went up the steps.

Those words coming from Niya's mouth were like a bullet by itself. Niya and the twins were his family in his eyes, and always had been. As bad as he wanted to run after Niya, he couldn't right now, he just had to worry about getting Zion back.

"Detective... we've got Niya and Tiffany leaving Niya's house, and it appears that Tiffany has a large caliber rifle in her possession. Possibly an AK-47," the surveillance officer told Det. Butler over the radio.

"Do not engage... I repeat, do not engage," Butler yelled over the radio.

With the right lawyer, Tiffany wasn't gonna be facing that much time for the rifle. Butler thought that it was best that they just let her go for now, instead of risking the possibility of being exposed. It would be hard to investigate someone who knows that they are being watched by the police. It was still early in the investigation. Time was the only thing Butler was counting on having, and the more time MHB had, the deeper they were gonna dig their own graves.

Dead silence took over the apartment. Gwen sat on the couch holding an icepack over her face from the bruise Dollaz left after knocking her out. Chad sat at the kitchen table with his head in his hands, waiting for the phone to ring. The abductors wrote in the note that they would be calling later on that night with instructions on how to get their son back. Chad had so many questions to ask, he didn't know where to start with Gwen. At this moment he really didn't even want to talk to her.

The loss of Zion had drained him so much, he ran out of tears to cry. He just wanted his son back, and the only person that could make that happen was sitting on the couch with a dumb look on her face. As much as he wanted to fuck Gwen up for putting his son's life in jeopardy, he just didn't have the energy to do it.

The dumb look Gwen had on her face wasn't because she felt stupid. She was sitting there trying to figure out who would be so stupid to do something like this for Mayo. Gwen really wanted to kill everything breathing for the return of her son, but she hadn't the slightest clue where to start. Mayo was still in jail, and just about everybody he knew in the streets turned their backs on him.

All Gwen and Chad could do was wait for the phone call, something that seemed like it would never happen, until it finally did. Gwen's cell phone rang so loud, it echoed throughout the whole apartment. Chad picked his head up to see Gwen grabbing the phone off the table. She looked at the phone, then looked over at Chad, and then back at the phone. She had a feeling it was them because of the blocked number. This was the call they both were waiting for.

"Hello..."

TO BE CONTINUED